NAKED CAME THE ROBOT

BARRY B. LONGYEAR

POPULAR LIBRARY

An Imprint of Warner Books, Inc.

A Warner Communications Company

Any resemblance that you might see between the characters in this book and real folks is probably something you might want to discuss with your analyst. Most of those who might have reason to feel offended by this work are already dead. The evidence I've seen would suggest that the rest of them can't read anyway.

POPULAR LIBRARY EDITION

Copyright © 1988 by Barry B. Longyear
All rights reserved.

Popular Library®, the fanciful P design, and Questar® are registered trademarks of Warner Books, Inc.

Cover design by Don Puckey
Cover illustration by Les Edwards

Popular Library books are published by
Warner Books, Inc.
666 Fifth Avenue
New York, N.Y. 10103

A Warner Communications Company

Printed in the United States of America

First Printing: November, 1988

10 9 8 7 6 5 4 3 2 1

DEDICATION

Naked Came The Robot is dedicated to the (herein) unnamed Maine State legislator who, in the midst of incredible national and local despair, unemployment, and recession, proposed a bill to have the dome on the statehouse in Augusta covered in gold. The funding of this enterprise was to be provided on a voluntary basis by the citizens of Maine. A campaign was to be launched to encourage all Mainers to turn in all of their unwanted gold to the state. This excess gold then would be turned into gold leaf and applied to the state dome by local smiths. Unlike the bill establishing Chester Greenwood Day, honoring the Farmington inventor of the earmuff, the glitter dome bill never got anywhere, so we just keep on piling up the surplus gold in backyards from Madawaska to Kittery. Still, it rests in fond memory as a sparkling example of the spirit of American political economy in action.

This work is also dedicated to: Jack Williamson (who gave me some advice at Windycon that has kept me sane and happy since); Harry Harrison, Jr. (for writing *Bill, the Galactic Hero*); Harlan Ellison (whom I never met, but he gave me a couple of chuckles and once put me in one of his stories, so I dropped him in here a couple of times); Kevin O'Donnell, Jr. (for giving up farming); Joel Rosenberg (for giving up disemboweled tribbles); and to Steve Perry (for laughing at me when I told him I got the Nebula).

O N E

Ft. Calley, Texas

CADET Sergeant Henry Fleming had a passion to enlist in the Economy. Tales of great deals hummed from the telescreens, and his eager eyes absorbed the marketing strategies, new products, bankruptcies, and graph-illustrated developments and he longed to see it all for real. His imagination painted for him wall-screen-sized pictures, opulent in sixty-toned graphics, lurid in deeds of breathless profit.

But his mother discouraged him. She would return after a hard day of pushing troops at the company, where she was first sergeant, kick off her boots, toss her uniform blouse over the back of the couch, and slouch down with her first beer of the night before the telescreen. She would scoff at the newscasters as they spoke with great ardor and patriotism of America's marketing inroads, Gross National Product advancement, and relative currency gains.

"Hosshit. Henry, jes' listen t' thet dim-ditty blowin' itall from 'is bunghole. Gawd, but it'd be love t' have thet blow-dried twat in fer comp'ny drills. I'd take t' starch outten 'is prangdoodle."

"Ma, I want to enlist in the Economy."

She crushed her empty beer can, tossed it across the room, and opened another can. Her gaze remained fixed on the telescreen. "Don't talk like a damn fool, Henry." She put the edge of the can to her lips and drank deeply. The discussion was at an end.

However, late that night in his room, his tele crackled with the news of the latest Soviet offensive in Western Europe. Everything from new Volga autos to GUM shoes were appearing in showrooms and stores. The low, low prices had Europeans diving for their charge cards. Economic commentators were agreed that the Soviets were selling below cost, dumping in an attempt to drive the U.S., Japan, and the Allies out of the European market.

Henry listened to a generated image of I. P. Daley, President of Boeing-Boeing–Serta Inner-Spring Mattresses, Inc., speak to the viewers about the new challenge from the east, and how American business and labor—the nation's economic big guns—were responding to the unprovoked attack. Daley's message was followed by a civilian recruiting spot. A tall, white-haired man sporting a goatee, wearing black silk top hat, striped trousers, swallow-tailed black coat, and wing-tipped collar complete with diamond-studded cravat, shook his gold-headed walking stick at the viewers and, with steely eye aglint, demanded: "Daddy Warbucks wants you for the U.S. Economy!"

After removing his bridge and brushing his teeth, all that night awake and in his dreams, visions of glory paraded in the dark, the sight of it blinding his mind's eye to his Army home. The next morning as he passed his mother's room on his way to morning formation, she looked up from where she was sitting on her footlocker spit shining her boots. "'Mornin', Henry."

"Good morning, Ma." Henry looked down. "Ma, about last night—"

"Don't want t' hear no more 'bout it, boy. Y' got a good life in t' Army. Any boy with a lick o' sense 'd know thet." She paused, moved the cigar from the left side of her mouth to the right side, and nodded at her son. "Don't fergit yer 'pointment t' git yer bridge fixed. Run along now t' formation, 'n' put thet fool notion outten yer haid."

TWO

The Old Soldier

THE Air was thin and chilly, the sun sharp and bright, as Henry trudged toward his battalion quadrangle, his brow furrowed. Enlisting was the right thing to do, he was certain. What if everybody left it all up to the robots? What then? Russia would have America's back against the economic ropes, that's what. But could he disobey his mother?

He thought of his mother. She still carried the memory and the pain of the Sarge, his father, in her heart. The Sarge had enlisted years before at the beginning of the Great Dog-food Wars and had made a bundle investing in Alpo-Dow. Henry had been barely old enough to understand the terrible news when it came. The recombinant DNA labs at Rolls-Royce Horsemeat Ltd. had announced the introduction of its vat-grown Dobbin-On-A-Stick, crushing the competition. Purina-Mitsubishi caved in first, taking the rest of the industry down with it. In despair, unable to face either his family or his creditors, the Sarge had climbed to the top of Hackensack's Disney-Playboy Tower, had let his tear-smeared gaze rest for a moment upon the distant Manhattan Wasteland, then plunged to his death upon the corner of Hefner & Tinkerbell. Ever since, Henry's mother had been against the Economy. She wanted him to go on to the United

States Military Academy's campus at Paducah, get his commission, and settle down in a cushy admin position on the general staff.

The youth paused and saw that his clouded mind had steered his footsteps to Ft. Calley's NCO club on the corner of Blood & Guts. The Old Soldier would be inside, his hands clasped around his cup of coffee, his unseeing gaze leveled on the club's robo performer. The Old Soldier was a veteran, having seen economic service in both the Dogfood Wars and the Sony–Gloria Stevens Robot Aerobics Revolt before reentering the Army in the Senior Service.

Henry quickly glanced down Guts to the clock-sign rotating over the branch office of the First Military Payline & Soldier's Fund. He still had a few minutes before morning formation. He pushed open the door. The darkness, thick smoke, and deafening music swallowed him. As his eyes adjusted to the dark he could make out the gleaming rows of bottles behind the bar. At the back of the room was a small stage where an overly padded USObot belted out "Monday, Monday" accompanied by the speakers mounted in her belly. There were only a few soldiers seated at the tables, and Henry looked for that familiar gleaming tower of stripes. Off to the left against the wall, far away from the others, he found the Old Soldier, the wrinkled black of his skin contrasting with the starched khaki of his uniform.

He walked over and came to attention next to the old man's table. As his heels clicked, the Old Soldier brought his thoughts back from his past and aimed his cloudy brown eyes at Henry. His face radiated power, hate, and Ultimate Disgust.

"You little pussy-whipped mama's boy. Where are you from, boy?"

"Texas, sir."

"There's only two things that come from Texas, boy: steers and queers. I don't see any horns on you, so you must be queer. Are you queer, boy?"

"Sergeant-Major Boyle, sir, can we cut this short? I only have a few minutes before I have to be at formation."

The Sergeant Major's eyebrows went up. "Sure, Fleming." He held out his hand toward the chair to his right. "Sit down. What's the problem?"

Henry pulled out the chair and sat down. He couldn't quite meet Sergeant Major Boyle's glance. "Sergeant Major, I've been thinking about joining up."

Boyle's eyebrows came back down as the old man returned his glance to his coffee cup. "Oh?"

"Yes sir."

"Henry, what's your mother think about you enlisting in the Economy? Have you mentioned it to her?"

The youth shrugged. "I told her, but you know my Ma. She's dead set against it. Because of the Sarge."

The old man nodded his shaved head. He took a sip of coffee, lowered the cup to the saucer, and faced the youth. "How can I help you, Fleming?"

"You were in the Economy, weren't you?"

The old man turned his attention back to his cup of coffee. "You know I was."

Henry leaned forward, his elbows upon the edge of the table. "What was it like?"

"I don't like to talk about it." He slowly shook his head. "I never talk about it." His head stopped shaking. "You don't know what it was like during the Revolt. The Army didn't support the economic effort. When me and my buddies came home from the Mall to the quadrangle we were treated like boots." He looked at Henry with pain-glazed eyes. "Like *boots*!"

The youth placed a gentle hand upon the old man's arm. "This isn't the Revolt, Sergeant Major. This is new business."

The Old Soldier pulled his arm away from Henry's grasp. "Business shmisness! The goddamned civilians promised me that my slot in the Army would be protected and that I would be put back in charge of my robot company when I was laid off. Ha! What they did was to give some wet-eared four-striped slacker my command! And me? Me they dump into the Senior Service! The Boneyard Brigade!" He shook his head slowly. "Me and those other vets from the Revolt don't attend those self-help groups to laugh about the good old days, I can tell you that, cadet."

"Sergeant Major, times have changed—"

"Changed?" The old man's nostrils flared as his breath snorted in hot blasts. He calmed down a bit, shook his head and picked up his coffee. "No one could tell me anything either."

"Sergeant—"

"Button it up, Fleming. I want to listen to Sue Baru." The old man turned his attention toward the stage as the robot shifted down into "Night Train" and began unbolting her plates, revealing pulsating mounds of cosmetic vinyl.

Henry wanted to try again, but thought better of it. The Old Soldier's mind had drifted away, back to his old command. It was time to get to formation anyway. Henry pushed back his chair and got to his feet. "I'll be seeing you, Sergeant Major."

The old man nodded slightly, his gaze still riveted on Sue Baru's perambulating pistons. The youth looked down at the floor and shuffled toward the door, his mind in turmoil.

THREE

The Quadrangle

BEFORE The 116th Cadet Battalion formed on the Ft. Calley, Texas, quadrangle, the cadets were buzzing with the news of the Soviet offensive and the intense business recruiting program that had been begun to help meet it. Cadet Corporal Doxie Millikin was showing her enlistment papers to her friends. She had signed up in the Economy the day before. "I'm supposed to report this afternoon to pick up my civvies."

She virtually glowed with self-importance. Private Neely squinted against the brilliance and asked, "Doxie, what about graduation? It's only another two months."

She assumed a stern expression and spoke with a voice hoary with countless campaigns. "Neely, in two months this country could be out of business. Now, how does a Cadet Corps graduation stack up against that?"

"Ya think so, Doxie?" Private Enid Weems looked up at her hero with large frightened eyes. "Could we go ... *bankrupt?*"

Doxie placed a hand on Enid's shoulder and gave it a comforting squeeze. "Not if I have anything to say about it." Her proud, confident expression aimed itself in Henry's direction. "What about you, Fleming? You're old enough. Are you going to sign up today?"

The youth's face turned red and he looked down. "I can't. I have an appointment with the dentist. Besides, my Ma——"

"You don't need your mother's permission."

Private Weems looked from Doxie to Henry. "Golly, if I was old enough, I sure would."

Several cadets from the platoon, two of them from Henry's squad, made a pact to go off base and enlist immediately following afternoon drill.

The cadet battalion adjutant issued the command to fall in. There was a brief moment of movement as the boys and girls found their places, dressed, and covered. Then there were three companies of erect youths. Sharply the reports were given, and as the adjutant took the reports and read out the orders for the day, Henry's face burned with shame.

FOUR

A Few Good Executives

LATE That afternoon, Henry was downtown standing nervously before the recruiter. The man was smartly dressed in a three-piece gray suit with a wine-red cravat. The cravat and his expensively manicured fingers sported gold-mounted diamonds of a size and quantity just within the bounds of good taste. Behind the recruiter's desk was one of the usual "Daddy Warbucks Wants You for the U.S. Economy" posters. Next to the Warbucks poster was another poster depicting an expensively dressed, handsome youth behind an expanse of highly polished walnut set in an office made almost entirely of glass. The magnificent view through the windows was of some major industrial center in full production, the skies black from the belching chimneys of mighty furnaces. Standing next to the young man was a voluptuous young woman clad only in tight-fitting mini jumper and steno pad. The poster stated quietly, but firmly

MERRILL LYNCH HONDA
IS LOOKING FOR
A FEW GOOD EXECUTIVES

Henry had thought long and hard about the company he

would join. All of the companies served the effort, but Merrill Lynch Honda was the elite. At least, that was the reputation the firm had among Henry's friends. Their motto was inscribed in gold on the front of the recruiter's desk: "The Few, The Proud, The Rich—And That's No Bull!"

The first in, the first out, the first to make a buck. Henry's breast swelled with pride. The recruiter shook Henry's hand, seated him in a leather-covered overstuffed chair, gave him a Macho-Panatela cigar, held out a light from a diamond-crusted cigar lighter, and with his other hand poured a double martini in a Waterford crystal tumbler.

"So, Mr. Fleming, you're interested in our little firm, are you?"

Henry choked on the cigar smoke, gagged on the martini, and nodded. "I want to join the best. Yes sir."

"This isn't the Army, Mr. Fleming. Just call me Arnold."

"Certainly . . . Arnold." Henry saw the recruiter's eyebrows rise in expectation. "Uh, call me Henry."

Arnold smiled warmly. "Thank you, Henry." The recruiter looked down at the forms Henry had filled out. "I see that you were accepted at U.S.M.A. at Paducah."

"Yessir—uh, that's right, Arnold. I know my application to the firm would look better if I had graduated—"

Arnold held up a hand. "Henry, right now you have no bad habits that we need to correct. You're a clean slate, and the firm likes clean slates." The recruiter looked over the forms again. "Your test scores are higher than average . . . *and* you've expressed an interest in going on to the Harvard Business School." Arnold's eye contact conveyed intense admiration. "That shows the proper spirit." The eye contact shifted to man-to-man. "We want tigers in the penthouse, Henry."

"Right, Arnold." Henry looked down at his martini, now half consumed. He puffed on the cigar, leaned back in the chair, and relaxed. This is going to be all right, he reflected.

"Here is your key to the executive washroom, your membership card and key to the worldwide chain of Fondle-bunny Clubs, the keys to your company car—a Honda Silver Streak, of course—and the keys to your company jet."

Henry nodded. This *is* going to be all right, he concluded.

Arnold pushed some papers across his desk. "Now, Henry, if you would autograph these, heh, heh."

Henry sipped at his martini as he leaned forward and squinted at the papers. "Whad're thoshe?"

"A mere formality. The firm prefers a simple handshake, but the law is the law. This is your contract with the firm. You needn't bother with the fine print." He flipped past an attached microfiche and pointed at another form. "This one is a minor requirement of the government's. It shows that you understand that after your contract date, you will no longer be eligible for any government medical, housing, education, employment, or welfare benefits."

Henry's eyebrows went up. What if I get sick, he thought. "I don't know—"

"Henry, what they say about business—that it's dog eat dog out there—is true. But Merrill Lynch Honda doesn't employ dogs. We are tigers—and that's no bull. It's the survival of the fittest, Henry, and we"—Arnold pointed up at the poster—"are the fittest."

Henry's head swam as he followed the direction of Arnold's finger. *The Few, The Proud, The Rich.* And it seemed to Henry's eyes that the pretty woman standing next to the young executive had removed her minijumper and was now sitting on the young man's lap.

Henry signed.

Arnold reached out and swept the keys and membership cards into his desk drawer. "We'll keep these safe for you, Henry, just until you reach Executive Level." Arnold stood and held out his hand. "Welcome to the firm. Let's do lunch sometime."

Henry shook the recruiter's hand, left his Waterford crystal glass on the desk, the cigar butt in the ashtray, and—halfway home—his martini on the sidewalk.

FIVE

Adieu, Ft. Calley

WHEN He returned home he passed through his mother's company area. He saw her standing in front of the Second Platoon barracks, reaming out a brindle recruit. Four other recruits stood at attention, waiting their turns.

"Ma, I've enlisted."

There was a short silence. Without turning from the object of her exorcisms, she said, "Hain't thet t' goddamn way?" She then continued reaming the brindle recruit.

On his contract day, when he stood in the doorway with his issue three-piece suit on his back, the grip of his black issue attaché case in his hand, with the gleam of adventure and profit in his eyes, he had seen two tears putting down their tracks on his mother's closely shaven cheeks.

Still, she had disappointed him by failing to ask him to send her money, or at least to send for her when he became rich and powerful. He had rehearsed in his mind for a beautiful farewell scene on the front porch. But she destroyed his plans by doggedly polishing her brass, smoking her cigar, and by her words.

"Now, you watch out, Henry, and take keer of yerself in thet business world. Don't go thinkin' y' kin bankrupt the hull So-veet economy at the start, 'cause y' cain't. Yer jest one little dollar-whomper 'mongst a hull bunch o' tother dollar-whompers, 'n' y' keep yer mouth shut 'n' follow orders.

"I din't get t' be no top kick by not knowin' which end my pisscutter covered. I packed bootblack 'n' brass polish in thet little fairy case o' yourn, 'n' some C rations. I want m' boy to be is sharp is any feather merchant on t' block, 'n' when y' run out, y' go 'n' write me fer more, so's I kin screw 'em outten the supply sergeant.

"'N' be careful who y' pick fer comp'ny. There's a stomp-full lot o' route-step meatbeaters out there on Civvy Street, Henry. Civilian life makes 'em wild, and they like nothin' better'n leadin' a young troop like you, such as never been away from 'is mother, 'n' fillin' 'is head with a load o' hosshit. You keep clear o' them cods, Henry. I don't want y' t' do anythin' I'd throw yer ass in t' stockade fer. Jest think like I was on yer tail ever' second 'n' yer'll come out o' it all right.

"'N' right in front o' yer haid, Henry, y' keep t' remembrance o' t' Sarge, yer pappy. He never stiffed a bartender, never got caught cheatin' at poker, 'n' he never hit a man he didn't hate.

"I don't know what else to tell y', Henry, 'cept never do less'n yer share on my account. If a time come when y' have t' lose yer shirt er do somethin' crooked, don't think o' nothin' but what's right, 'cause there's many o' top soldier like me who has t' go up agin' sech things time 'n' time 'n' the Army'll take keer o' us all. So long, Henry. Watch out 'n' be a good boy."

Of course he had been impatient under the ordeal of this speech. Not only hadn't it been what he had expected, he could only understand every third word. He departed feeling vaguely confused relief. Still, when he looked back from the gate he had seen his mother toss her cigar into a butt can as she lowered herself into her rocking chair. Her brown face, upraised, was streaked with tears, and her hand trembled as it reached for another beer. He bowed his head and went on, feeling suddenly ashamed.

From home he went to the quadrangle to bid farewell to the battalion. They thronged about him with envy and admiration, praising the cut of his three-piecer, timidly begging to touch the softly glowing imitation leather of his attaché case. He felt the growing gulf between him and his uniformed mates and he filled his spine with ever-increasing self-importance. He and some of his fellows who had arrived before morning formation wearing civvies were overwhelmed by the attention. But the adulation was cut short by the adjutant falling in the battalion and by the MPs chasing them all off the military installation. Ft. Calley, Texas, was behind them. The future for Henry was Merrill Lynch Honda headquarters in Piscataway, New Jersey.

SIX

The Last War and The Wealth of Nations

THE Dawn light struggled through the grimy windows of the train car, touching the closed eyes of a few of the recruits. As they awakened, the noise they made caused the remainder to pull back their minds from soft dreams of executive banquets and frolics in money bins bursting with bank notes.

Henry rubbed the grit from his eyes and tried to quiet the rumble from his empty stomach as he looked for Doxie Millikin and the others from his battalion who had enlisted. He didn't see them. Instead there was the husky blond athlete, the practical joker, the slick gambler, the callow farmboy, the tough street punk, the kid with a guitar, the eager beaver, and the guy with his nose in a book. The conductor entered the car and began folding them up. They were made out of cardboard.

The image of the guy with his nose in a book moved. The head turned, glanced at him, and smiled. "It's to keep up your morale."

"What?"

He nodded toward the conductor. "The familiar faces of the cardboard company. You know, from the old war movies on the tele."

"The only tele I watch is the Rukeyser network business news." Henry reached a hand across the aisle. "Fleming, Henry."

The man shook his hand. "Bach, Phil. Just call me Phil. Who'd you sign up with, Fleming?"

"Call me Henry. I'm with Merrill Lynch Honda."

Phil withdrew his hand and placed his book on the seat next to him. "I'm with Bache-Caterpillar. Did you know that after The Last World War in 1999 just about the only governmental structure left intact was the military?"

"Say, what?"

"The Last World War (8:26 A.M.–9:53 A.M., April 1, 1999)," Phil said parenthetically, "was no more an end to human global conflict than World War I was the war to end war. But just as the Great War saw planted the seeds of warfare between machines that flowered into the next war's bomber and missile filled skies, The Last War saw the death of armed might, nuclear or otherwise, as an acceptable instrument of any nation's foreign policy. Before The Last War was even two hours old, before the first mushrooms over New York, London, Moscow, and Peking had dissipated, a planet-wide consciousness seemed to grip the world's governments with the power of humanity itself, saying, We have had enough."

Henry rubbed his chin, suspecting that he might have missed something. "You don't say."

Phil nodded. "The messages heard by the remaining fragments of the world's governments from their peoples, almost always organized into angry mobs, were the same: There will be no more war. Whatever your ambition, philosophy, ideology, bias, thirst, or passion—find some other way. Take your fingers off of the buttons, declare victory, blame or pay off whoever, do whatever it is that you have to do to save face, but stop the bombs and missiles. There will be no more war."

"That seems like a pretty good idea, Phil," said Henry, attempting to participate.

"Unfortunately, Henry, while long enough to eliminate almost forty percent of the human race's industrial and agricultural capacity, The Last World War was too brief to eliminate more than ten percent of the humans. Overnight Earth went from a war economy to no economy. Economic depression of a degree and scale never before imagined blighted every aspect of human existence and aspiration." The man seated across the aisle sadly shook his head.

"The problems were of staggering proportions. In the United States of America alone, unemployment rapidly moved above sixty percent. This could have only been made worse by dismantling a thirty-four-million-man armed force that no longer had any function. Welfare, unemployment compensation, social security, medicare, public parks, and countless other governmental programs and institutions Americans counted on for protection from bad economic times had been crippled. Records were fragmented, entire offices and staffs were particles of ash suspended in the atmosphere."

"So," Henry yawned and slouched back in his seat. "What'd they do?"

"With the constantly increasing expenses of now-useless weaponry subtracted, it cost only a tenth as much to keep a soldier and his family in the service as it did to support an unemployed worker and his family on Civvy Street. Also, soldiers functioning under the Uniform Code of Military Justice were a whole lot less trouble than hungry civilians with time heavy on their hands. In the United States the weaponry was dismantled, but the men and women of all of the branches of the now disarmed forces were kept on the payroll."

"But—"

"Hunger, the lack of work, and sheer despair picked up enlistments, and special programs were instituted that enabled entire families to join the service on the family version of the 'buddy plan.' Children and teens became members of the Cadet Corps, while those over sixty became members of the Senior Service. With the pressures of military spending, education, welfare, and so on decreased, income and corporate taxes were reduced to half, then to a third of prewar levels. With this pressure removed from the civilian economy, business and industry began booming."

"No fooling?" said Henry as he frantically searched for a graceful exit.

Phil Bach leaned toward Henry, his face gripped with a horrible calm. "At the end of the second year after the war, the GNP showed a startling eleven percent increase over the last year before the war. The next year saw an even more dramatic increase. Everyone, including those in the military, were either comfortable or downright wealthy. Unemployment stood at zero percent. Hunger, inadequate medical care, and poor educational opportunities became socio-historic dinosaurs. Violent and white-collar crime dropped to levels of statistical insignificance." Phil grinned as he leaned back and clasped his hands in satisfaction. "With the rise in incomes there was an increased interest in robotic stand-ins to free humans for more leisure activities."

"That sure is something, Phil," Henry yawned. "Where—"

"Other governments saw what America had done and rapidly followed suit. In the span of only a few years, the world saw prosperity and the birth rate began to decrease. The population projections prompted startling increases in the production of industrial, commercial, and domestic robots. The results were more jobs at higher wages and shorter hours. The human race had finally found the corner around which prosperity lurked. By the year 2015, three out of every five babies opened their eyes in the infantry. By the year 2022, to become a civilian one either had to have been born into a civilian family or had to enlist from the military into civilian service. And now, in 2042, the Econ—"

"I'm sorry for interrupting," apologized Henry as he reached across the aisle and yanked the man's necktie, moving Phil's complexion toward the blue end of the spectrum. "But why are you telling me all this?"

Phil removed the hand from his neckwear, his expression one of injured patience. "If you don't understand what I've just told you, Henry, the rest of this will simply make no sense at all."

The man neated up his necktie, picked up his book, and resumed reading. The book's title was *The Wealth of Nations* by A. Smith.

Henry's stomach rumbled again and he remembered the C rations his mother had packed in his attaché case. Placing it upon his lap, he opened it and selected mule morsels in brown gravy. As he gnawed he paged through the copy of his contract. What he could read seemed fairly straightforward; he could make out nothing on the microfiche.

The youth folded up the form and placed it into his inside coat pocket. He closed his case and continued to gnaw as he looked through the window at the black skies and eternal pyres of the Burning Tulsa Desert. But his eyes did not see the oil field fires that had been ignited during the minutes of The Last War. Instead he dreamed of glass towers, power, and wealth.

Wealth.

The Wealth of Henry Fleming, he mused. The youth smiled and glanced at the book in Phil Bach's hands. *The Wealth of Nations*. It's a great title, thought Henry. I wonder what it's about?

SEVEN

Look for
the Union Label

"LET'S Go, Slug! The Movement is waiting!"

Henry opened his eyes, revealing the familiar interior of the railiner car. Outside it was night. Monstrously large men with clubs were storming up and down the aisle, growling at the recruits, herding them into the aisle, shoving them out of the car. One of the monsters was leaning over Henry's seat. He reached out a huge hand and grabbed the youth's arm.

"Kissy, kissy, Sleeping Beauty. Let's go."

Henry pulled away. "What's this? I'm not going with you!"

The man grinned, revealing twin rows of teeth filed into sharp points. "Don't go scabbie on me, laddie."

"Scabbie? I have to report to Piscataway for—"

The man succeeded in renewing his grip on Henry's arm. "Slug, you *have* reported." He pulled the lad into the aisle and pushed him toward the end of the car. The other trainees were looking about, wide-eyed and frightened.

The youth was shoved out into the night. His knees scraped as they hit the roadbed. "Up, young slug." A hand pulled him to his feet. "This ain't the Army, slug. Now you gotta work for a livin'."

The man's hand pushed him away from the railiner toward the end of a line of terrified trainees. The big men flanked both sides of the line, the clubs in their hands at the ready. Henry took his place, silently noting the damage to his sharply cut three-piece suit. If he ever managed to get away from this collection of thugs, he would look a sight when he reported. The line moved rapidly. There was a man sitting at a table, a tiny transceiver in his left hand. As the boy in front of Henry was pushed roughly toward a lone car resting on a siding, more rough hands pushed Henry in front of the table.

"Name?"

Henry's throat felt very dry. "Henry. Henry Fleming."

"Who signed you up?"

Henry responded with a puzzled expression. "What's going on?"

Something struck Henry between his shoulder blades, driving him to his knees. Dazed, he gripped the edge of the table and looked at the man.

"Your contract, slug. What company?"

Henry smiled. Perhaps some sense would be made out of this after all. The youth pulled himself to his feet, stood erect, his chest swelling with pride. "Sir, my contract is with Merrill Lynch Honda."

The man spoke into his transceiver. "Fleming, Henry. More bull." He lowered the instrument and nodded at someone behind Henry. The youth found himself shoved toward the railiner car. He walked the few steps, was shoved up the stairs and into the car.

It was brightly lit, a platform at the end nearest Henry, rows of chairs facing the platform filling the remainder of the car. Several of the chairs were filled with men and women. Next to the platform was a podium, and behind the podium stood a slender fellow in a white suit with a wide-brimmed white hat. His upper lip sported a thin black mustache and the glow of the terminal screen in the podium cast ghostly shadows on his face.

Henry was pushed up on the platform and the man in the white suit began, "Now here's a fine-looking lad." The man in white looked down at his screen. "Henry Fleming, eighteen years old, former cadet sergeant squad leader, two months short of graduating secondary. He is under a standard bull contract. What am I bid?"

"Two hundred," shouted a voice from the back, and Henry watched in horror, realizing he was being auctioned off.

The man in white pointed at the back of the car. "Velvet Bruce's Sporting Palace bids two."

"Three," shouted another voice.

"Eye-bam-oh bids three. Do I hear four?"

"Cztery!"

"Associated Salt Mines of Warsaw bids four. Five? Do I hear five?"

"Five!"

"Eye-bam-oh bids five. Do I hear six? Do I hear six? Five-fifty? Five-twenty-five? Come, now, folks. At five and a quarter, I'd buy the piece of meat myself for a dart target."

"Five-twenty-five!"

"Five and a quarter to Velvet Bruce. He's a looker, all right." He faced Henry. "Turn around once, boy. Go ahead."

Henry turned around and the man in white continued his patter. "Velvet sees a good thing here, but the old ladies'd like a piece of this. Let's hear a bid from Gerry Active."

"Okay," replied a horribly ugly old hag. "Five and a half."

"Gerry Active goes five and a half. Do I hear six? Six? Five-seventy-five?"

"Five-seventy-five!"

"Eye-bam-oh bids five and three quarters. Do I hear six? Six?" A brief moment of silence. "Going once. Twice. Sold to Eye-bam-oh for five and three quarters. Pay the cashier and collect your meat. Next we have a pretty little . . ."

Henry was led off the platform and back out into the night. He was led away from the car and over to a small gathering. When he came closer he noticed that the center of the gathering contained around a dozen of the boys and girls he had been with on the train. The edge of the gathering was composed of club-swinging thugs.

One of the men at the edge talked to someone behind Henry. "Is that the last of our quota?"

"Yeah, Spikes. We might as well hang cards on 'em and call it a night."

The one addressed as Spikes faced the gathering. He stood silently for a moment and then spoke. "My name is Spikes. You will call me Brother Spikes. Your contracts have been sold to Eye-bam-oh, and until you are assigned to your apprentice programs, I am your representative." Hands again shoved Henry where he didn't want to go until he was standing in front of a table. Spikes held out his hand.

"Name and money."

"I'm Henry Fleming. What am I supposed to be paying you for?"

"Dues, boy."

"Dues?"

"Union dues, Fleming. You think you got a free ride out here? You're not back on the quadrangle, slug. This is the Economy."

"How much are the dues, Bro—Brother Spikes?"

A rough hand reached into Henry's coat, snatched his wallet, and tossed it on the small table. Spikes pulled out the bills, and shook his head as he counted the money.

"This ain't even enough for a down payment." Spikes shoved the bills into his own pocket and handed a plastic card to Henry. "There's your union card, Brother Fleming. You still owe seventy-one dollars dues for this month. The union hall's address is on the card. You got no seniority and you're not paid up, so you got no privileges, fringes, protections, or benefits. Right now Eye-bam-oh is on strike, so you got no job, and you're new, so you can't draw from the strike fund. Get yourself a place to stay and have your robot report to the union hall at six sharp tomorrow morning for picket duty. Any questions?"

"I don't have a robot."

"I want a body on the line, brother. If you don't own one, use your own."

"Mr. Spikes—"

"Brother Spikes."

"Brother Spikes, I don't get any of this. I joined Merrill Lynch Honda and I expected to be—"

Spikes and several of the others issued dirty chuckles. Someone in the darkness made a crack about Fondlebunnies and the keys to the executive washroom. Spikes grinned.

"So, Brother Fleming, you had thoughts about cornering the world markets with a bare little bimbim 'pon your knee, did you?"

"Well . . ." As a matter of fact, Brother Spikes had accurately summarized the general text of Henry's capitalistic visions.

"Brother Fleming, you didn't think you were going to start at the top, did you?" Spikes shook his head and his accomplices guffawed. "If you don't have any more questions—"

"Just one more question, Brother Spikes. What *is* Eye-bam-oh?"

"That's I-B-A-M-O. The International Brotherhood Associated of Medics and Orderlies. 'To Serve and To Heal.' Solidarity, brother, and we're all right, Jack. Now getcher scrawny butt outta here. Next."

Later that night Henry found out that the city he was walking through was Keynesburg, Ohio. By signing an agreement attaching his future wages, he obtained the use of a cold-water walk-up on Malthus Avenue. He shared the room with Johnny Morgan, a new union janitor in the Bache-Caterpillar Building. Johnny was fair-haired, slight of build, and regaled Henry to the early hours with his own business ambitions.

"Y' see, Henry, I ain't goin' t' be runnin' polishin' robots 'n' zappin' craphouse germs ferever. I got my eye on a clerkin' slot in t' boiler room. That's where the brokers buy 'n' sell t' hull world. By gum, Henry, I'd make me a crackerjack broker, I would."

Henry slept, dreaming of long cars, mahogany-paneled boardrooms, and bankrupt Soviet capitalists. There were the threads of a tune, a mournful melody, each refrain ending with "Comrade, can you spare a kopek?"

EIGHT

The Battle of
Keynesburg General

THE Next morning, Henry reported to the IBAMO union hall. Brother Spikes took him in tow, ushered him into a long, sleek, robot-chauffeured limo, and deposited him in front of the Keynesburg General Hospital.

Henry stood on the sidewalk. "Brother Spikes, just what am I supposed to do?"

Spikes pointed through the rear window at a crowd of robots gathered around the hospital's driveway. "Take yourself over there, Brother Fleming, and find Hugo. He's the line captain. He'll tell you what to do."

Henry turned in the direction indicated and the limo squealed off into the traffic. There was an oblong parade of two dozen rusty Mark Two robots treading across the hospital's entrance. Several other robots, on legs instead of treads, stood watching the pickets. Each picket robot carried a sign, and the aggregate of the signs accused Keynesburg General with treason, baby-killing, communist-buggering, child pandering, vampirism, and being unfair to organized labor. Those pickets whose tape loops were still operational would issue cries of "Unfair!" at measured intervals. One picket, whose loop was not in such good condition, kept saying, "'fair! 'fair!"

As he approached the line, Henry noticed several of the legged robots gathered around another legged robot. A few of the robots had their fingers stuck into the chest of what appeared to be the center of attention, while the robots farther away stood clicking and whirring.

One of the robots, with "Property of Channel Six Eyewitness News" stenciled on its can, pulled its finger out of the center robot's chest and said, "Thank you for the statement, Hugo."

The other news reporters removed their fingers from Hugo's chest and expressed their thanks. As they cleared away from the silver machine, Henry walked up. "Is your name Hugo?"

"Pissov," replied the robot.

Henry's face grew dark. "Say what?"

"Pissov," repeated the robot. "Hugo Pissov. That's *o-v* rather than *o-f-f*. Are you from IBAMO?"

Henry allowed his brow to cool a mite. "Yes."

The robot extended its right hand. "Let me see your card, brother."

The youth deposited his union card into Hugo's hand and watched as the machine inserted the plastic wafer into its chest.

"Mmmm." Hugo withdrew the card and returned it to Henry. "They just pulled you fresh off the train, eh, Brother Fleming?"

"That's right . . . uh. What do I call you? Brother Pissov?"

"No. I am an appliance. Only humans may belong to the labor movement, which should tell you a thing or two about the labor movement. I answer to either Hugo, Pissov, or Hugo Pissov. Before you ask, the name is the result of an attack of the cutes suffered by my first American owner, the late Adolph Schwartz, novelty item manufacturer specializing in phony dog crap with the brand name Sham-poo. I was manufactured in Pinsk."

"Pinsk?"

"A city in the White Russian Soviet Socialist Republic."

Henry took a step back. "Russian? But—"

"Put your mind at ease. I have been programmed for the union. I am completely loyal to motherhood, IBAMO, and the American Way, whatever that may be. Only my soul is Russian. What do you want?"

"Oh. I've been assigned to picket duty. Brother Spikes told me to ask you what I was supposed to do."

Hugo whirred for a moment. "You are the human line captain. Your official function is to supervise the operation and conduct of the mechanicals in the demonstration. Human supervision of mechanicals is required by the lackeys of the capitalistic dogs squatting in the state legislature, although this is the first time I ever had to put up with the genuine article. Can't you afford a robot of your own?"

The robot's sensors performed a vertical scan of Henry's stained and crumbling three-piecer. "I was a fool to ask." Hugo Pissov turned and faced the picket line.

"But what do I do?"

A speaker beneath the robot's right arm crackled at Henry. "What you do is what you are qualified for: stand there, keep out of trouble, and let me get on with my work."

"EXL-AX, pick up the pace!" Without turning back, Hugo walked up to a Mark Two that had slowed in its path, a grinding sound emanating from its base. Hugo lifted an arm, made a fist, and brought it down upon the head of the shorter machine. "I said move it, EXL-AX!" A *grunt*, a tiny puff of smoke, and the picket stopped dead, making a pitiful wa-wa-wa-wa sound.

Hugo appeared to go berserk. "Look at this flimsy hunk of inferior production! It is a testimonial to the ineptitude of Western engineering, manufacture, assembly, programming, operation, and maintenance!"

"Unfair," whimpered the picket.

"Bah!" Hugo tipped over the picket and kicked in its motor control package. "You fat Americans think you own the world! We will bury you!"

Henry strolled over and stopped next to the line captain. Hugo was jumping up and down upon the picket, reducing it to its component parts. "I don't mean to interrupt you while you're working, Hugo, but it's about this loyalty thing."

Hugo stepped from the rubble and faced the youth. "What about it, American pig?"

"It's the . . . well, it's the way you talk. It doesn't seem like the way a loyal American—"

"Congress shall make no law respecting an establishment of religion, or prohibiting the free exercise thereof; or abridging the freedom of speech, or of the press; or the right of the people peaceably to assemble, and to petition the Government for a redress of grievances." Hugo poked a finger at Henry's chest. "Is that red, white, and blue enough for you, dog drool? Believe this, bowel breath, my speech is one thing that I never allow anyone to abridge."

Henry rubbed his chest. The robot's fingers were sharp. "You're only a machine, Hugo. You don't have any rights."

"That's what Mister Charlie told blacks, Indians, and women. We shall overcome—" Hugo interrupted his tirade, periscoped his head up two meters, and swiveled his head about in a complete circle. Bringing his head down, Hugo turned toward the pickets and shouted, "Strike breakers! Defense formation! PAK-MN, VIC-20, BBC-WS, and MUN-GO, take the corners!"

Hugo strode in among the pickets, shoving, pointing, kicking. "Sometimes I wonder how I ever keep nut and bolt together! Get on line, you miserable garbage can! You! That's right, PIN-TO, the tired iron running around in circles! Get into position!"

As Hugo organized the pickets, the news-reporting machines hustled to positions with a good view of the coming fray, but well removed from danger. As they cleared the area, Henry noticed thirty tall green robots on the opposite side of the street. They were of a much chunkier build than even Hugo, and their hands carried lengths of pipe and chain, bricks, clubs, pipe wrenches, and screwdrivers. The pickets, having formed a union square, picket signs at the ready, became silent. Hugo stopped next to Henry and nodded in the direction of the green robots. "Look at the scab iron management is using now. Pretty, aren't they?"

"Hugo, are they Soviet?"

"No. Those are U.S. combat 'bots sold to the management. The government auctioned them off after the Last War. All the armaments have been removed, but they still have bad attitudes."

"What do we do?"

"I've already signaled for the police 'bots."

A roar came from the green robots, "DEATH TO EYE-BAM-OH!"

The pickets roared back, "UNFAIR! UNFAIR! UNFAIR!"

Hugo shook his head. "Limited programming. That's the way to go down to the junkyard, isn't it? With half-witted union slogans for a battle cry?"

Hugo faced the green machines and turned his volume up to maximum. "Ya mutha was a manure spreader!"

"Don't you think talk like that might make them angry, Hugo?"

"Piss off, Pissov!" answered one of the green robots.

Hugo sighed. "Such wit. Such originality." Up again went his volume. "Your mutha was buggered by an Armenian forklift!"

A brick sailed overhead and struck one of the pickets, knocking it over. The picket whistled and whimpered, "Unfair!" just before its lights went out.

Another picket began rushing across the street, shouting "Yougoddamnedunfair—"

"Get back in line!" ordered Hugo.

"They got JON-EE!"

"Get back!" The picket returned slowly to the line. Hugo strolled back and forth between the square and the green machines. "Steady, boys. That's what they want: to get you out there one at a time. Keep formation. The police'll be here soon."

The air and ground began trembling. Again Hugo's head periscoped up. "Ah, dammit!" His head came down and aimed at Henry. "Just what we needed."

"What is it, Hugo?"

"A crowd. Everybody in this lousy burg must have sent the family iron out to demonstrate. It looks like they're being egged on by some more 'bots from the Commie-Gong."

"Is that good or bad?"

Hugo's head spun in a complete circle. "Good or bad? Five hundred angry cement mixers are going to be on us in a few seconds, sworn to tear IBAMO sprocket from mainspring, and *you* want to know is that good or bad? Are American *humans* of substandard manufacture, too?"

"Okay!"

"Jeez."

"I *said* okay, Hugo!"

The green machines began moving, the clanks of their cast-metal footsteps shaking the ground. Henry's mouth was dry and he looked about for a safe spot. "Hugo, where should I be?"

"Get inside the square and hold the line. If I go down, take over and direct things from there."

The youth nodded and ran between two of the pickets into the center of the square. Measured, thunderously loud chanting came from the approaching crowd. "DEATH TO IBAMO! DEATH TO IBAMO!"

Walking over and crouching behind the corner picket named MUN-GO, Henry shouted out to Hugo, "What's the Commie-Gong, anyway?"

"Pro-Soviet robots against competition. They want us to just cave in and roll over in response to the Soviet challenge. I bet their owners are all holding Russian paper."

"Owners? They're all robots?"

"Would you be out here if you could afford to force some poor computerized coffee grinder to stand in for you? Not *all* humans are stupid." Pissov grabbed his stainless steel crotch and danced before the advancing wall of angry animated metal. "Hey, Robby the Robotovitch! I gotcher economy right here! Yaaaa, ha-hah!"

MUN-GO's back began ringing again and again. Henry opened a hinged panel there and picked up the telephone receiver that he found inside the compartment. "Hello?"

There was a familiar voice on the other end. "Henry?"

"Ma!"

"Gawd, 'tis love t' hear yer voice, Henry."

A piece of pipe whizzed by Henry's head. "It's good to hear you too, Ma."

"I jest called, boy, t' find out how' r ya doin, 'n' if yer orders come through 'n' all."

As the incoming-call indicator flashed above the hook in MUN-GO's back, Henry had to duck to miss being throttled by a length of whirling chain. "I'd love to talk to you some more, Ma, but I'm kind of busy. There's a call on my other line."

"Heh, boy, yer in the thick o' business already, eh?"

"You could say that, Ma."

"Henry, his yer office nice 'n' big?"

"It's big." Another brick whizzed by, bonging off of NIX-ON's jowl. "Ma, I really got to go. 'Bye."

"So long, Hen—"

The youth cut the connection and released the receiver as a Molotov cocktail shattered against NIX-ON's face, drenching that corner of the square in roaring flames. "Hello?"

"Brother Fleming?" It was Spikes.

"Yes?"

"Our records show you received a personal call on a union robot. First, I know you've only been in the brotherhood a few hours—"

"Brother Spikes, can I get back to you? Things—"

"Keep your trap shut, slug! When I'm ready to listen, I'll let you know!"

The crowd and the green machines charged. Henry dropped the receiver and backed away from the street side of the square. Several of the pickets were backing up, then one broke and sped for the safety of the hospital grounds. Henry, his heart choked with panic at the oncoming clanking horde, turned and ran after. Blindly, all of the dragons of death and imagination at his heels, the youth put his entire mind on escape, his entire effort into his legs pumping at the ground.

A picket rolled in front of him, coming to a halt in Henry's path. "Go back! You have to go back!" the picket cried.

The picket swung its sign at Henry's head, knocking him to the ground with a clang. Just before he lost consciousness, he realized that the signs weren't made from scrap lumber and posterboard. They were made with solid iron bars welded to boiler plate.

The world reappeared in fuzzy smears of violent sound and color. All he could think of was safety. Sanctuary. As he crawled off he heard Hugo crying out, "Stand fast, boys! Stand fast!"

Chains, bricks, and bent metal signs rained from the smoke-filled sky. The thunderous agony of metal punching the bejesus out of metal pummeled Henry's eardrums, the crashing mixed with the horrible yelling of the Commie-Gong. Henry crawled faster, into the street where the gutters ran with oil. He backed away, horrified at the greasiness on his hands. He stood, looked uphill through the smoke at some trees, and ran for them, his lungs and legs aching, his heart promising heaven anything it wanted if it would only allow him to find safety.

N i n e

Unfair!

ONCE Among some bushes, he groveled breathlessly against the ground, thankful that the sounds of battle had grown dimmer. When his breathing quieted, he heard voices coming from the opposite side of the bush. He gingerly stood in a crouch and looked around. He was on a gentle rise that gave a view of the carnage below. Hugo was nowhere to be seen, but the flaming shape of the square still held in the center of that angry crowd. The crowd was thinning, moving away from the pickets, falling back.

Henry felt as though he were in the center of the commission of a crime. The IBAMO pickets had triumphed after all.

"Here," said a voice. "It's all there. You don't have to count it."

Henry peered through the leaves and saw a dark-haired man in a blue suit glowering at a second man. The blue suit had two medals, in the shape of red stars, pinned to its left lapel. The second man's back was toward Henry.

The man in the blue suit thrust his hands into his coat pockets and fumed as he looked at the IBAMO pickets below. "Five hundred dollars. It's all there."

"I know, Vladimir, I know," replied the second man, stuffing a roll of green into his trouser pocket. "Do you want to put a little something down on the Farnsworth Nursing Home strike?"

"What if the union bosses accept the new contract?"

"Then all bets are off. Okay?"

The one called Vladimir glared with hateful eyes at the other. "It was unfair of you to have a human on the picket line."

The other man's shoulders shrugged as his hands went out in a gesture of innocence. "It was never agreed to." He chuckled. "But a dead piece of human meat'll sure give the media something to chew on, won't it?"

"At Farnsworth, will any humans be on the line? If I am going to wager, I want it understood that there are to be no humans."

The second man shook his head. "Naw. All we got there are picket robots."

"You are certain?"

"Sure."

Vladimir nodded. "Very well. I will wager a thousand."

The second man whistled. "Aren't you a little nervous about getting caught with your hand in the Commie-Gong till?"

"One thousand."

"Okay, you got a bet. Eight tomorrow morning at the nursing home?"

Vladimir nodded, turned, and walked to a waiting limo. It screeched off, leaving behind a cloud of dust and a happy man. The second man laughed lustily and slapped his big hands on his knees. "By gum, you commie bastard, I gotcha that time! Hooo-wheeee!"

After a little dance the man turned and headed for another black limo. When he turned, Henry saw his face. It was Brother Spikes. As the limo pulled away, Henry sat confused.

The wail of approaching police robots drowned every other sound.

Ten

The Dead Robot

HOURS Later, the sun sinking toward the horizon, Henry moved from the bushes to the thick woods. He felt angry, betrayed, his dreams of glory running down the storm drains along with the 10W30 of his mates on the picket line. His very first job in the Economy he had fled in terror, and the job had been performed anyway, and no thanks to Henry Fleming.

The roots and branches tugged at his arms and legs, switches swatted him in the face. After an hour of this, the space beneath the leaves growing darker, Henry sat on a fallen log, thankful that he was far away from the eyes of men.

What could he tell his mother? His heart grew cold and fragile at the thought of her eyes deeply hurt, her big boot working on his soft end, also deeply hurt.

But it was not the pain. It was the *lie* of business. Ever since his first game of Monopoly, the fame and glory of business had been paraded before him. Before he had died, his father, the Sarge, had given him his very own set of tin businessmen. Henry would spend hours moving them through dollhouse-sized offices, backstabbing tiny co-workers, filling miniature rooms with tiny bags of money, balling little toy secretaries on little toy couches.

He shook his head at his youthful fantasies. Reality was in the gutter in front of the Keynesburg General Hospital. More reality was sitting right in front of him.

He stood, horror-stricken, as he saw a thing.

He was being looked at by a dead robot who was seated with its back against a packing case full of cans, its amputated left leg cradled in its arms. The partially obscured lettering on the packing case said:

ADDIX.
When your robot's feeling low,
Just one can restores that glow.

The robot's grease and oil splattered casing was scorched, smoke-blackened, and dented. The visual sensors were shattered and black with lifelessness, and they stared at Henry from that rusted head, accusing him with silent transmissions—saying in measured ghostly syllables:

"Unfair! Unfair! Unfair!"

Henry stood, climbed over the log, and backed away from the apparition, convinced that if he turned his back on it for only a split second, the thing would spring at him. Farther and farther the youth retreated until he felt the unyielding presence of a tree at his back. He took one last look at the robot, turned, and fled more deeply into the darkening woods, the image of the rusting metal man wailing at his back.

ELEVEN

Pickets

H E Ran, jumping stumps and dodging trees, until he came to rest next to a chain-link fence. When the rasping of his breath eased, the distant sounds of a battle, the proportions of which dwarfed the little fracas in front of Keynesburg General, came to his ears. Management wasn't only trying to break IBAMO; assaults were taking place all across the city.

He walked along the fence until he found a place where part of it was down. He entered the grounds and walked warily toward the noise. The woods edged out on a rise overlooking a vast factory complex. Directly below him what appeared to be thousands of robots were locked in mortal combat. A large-scale reproduction of a battle between armies of ants: limbs and heads torn away, torsos hacked in half, the fit writhing in their fierce contest upon a blanket of the dead. It was a vast, roaring machine whose single purpose was the reduction of crafted metal to scrap. Surrounding the battle was a wall of deenergized union robots and robot bits. Sort of a picket fence, thought Henry.

Nearby was a shocking pink Mark Two guarding an automatic money machine that displayed an illuminated sign that said "Charge-Eze." The robot had Visa, Master-Card, and American Express stickers all over its can.

"What's happening?" the youth cried to the robot. The Mark Two simply wheeled purposefully around the charge machine. Henry pulled it to a halt. "Answer me! Why aren't you down there fighting with the rest? Why are you guarding this worthless machine?"

"I'm Charge-Eze's picket!" answered the Mark Two.

Covering his ears, Henry backed into the woods, turned, and ran for the fence. All sense of direction was lost, and he cried as he stumbled in blind panic for a safe place. In minutes he came to a place of smooth rolling hills, tiny numbered flags dotting the landscape.

The ground was torn and littered with debris. The torso and head of a robot was stretched on the closely cropped grass, the shaft and head of a six iron protruding from its left visual sensor. Next to it were the silent remains of a union robocart and a scabcart that had struggled to their deaths in a sand trap. Farther off were the motionless remains of several other robots, a pall of smoke settling over them.

Henry felt out of place. This part of the Economy was owned by the deenergized, and he hurried away before the ghosts of the broken machines rose, shouting "Unfair!" The space between his shoulder blades itched in anticipation of a barrage of divots, followed closely by ghostly nonnegotiable wage demands.

TWELVE

Hot Oil

H E Came finally to a road from which he could see in the distance pyres of flame and smoke and many-colored gangs of robots. In the road itself was a mangled, spark-sputtering, oil-squirting, smoking stream of robots moving away from the many battles.

One hopped along, carrying its own left leg in its arms. Its voice module kept up a constant r-r-rawk, r-r-rawk sound. One fumed from its neck, the head carried in its hands arguing loudly that the only reason it had been damaged was through the mismanagement of the union leadership. One would walk along with the traffic a few steps, whirl about, and walk against the traffic a few steps, then whirl again and repeat the maneuver, crying, "Charge it!" every time it turned.

One picket 'bot, its head half crushed, stumbled along, its words drawn from programming received before being purchased by some labor union. It was trying to sell Spring Herb Deodorant to the others, with lucrative competition-secure territories for those interested in becoming dealers.

The youth joined this parade and marched along with it. The animated rubble testified to the awful machinery of war, not to mention the war of machinery, in which the metal men had been engaged.

Tracked union carryalls moving fresh robots into the fray would race through the crowd sending already fragmented units scrambling for the safety of the shoulders. As the wounded hopped and crawled back to the road they would send the curses of all manufactured humanity after the vehicles.

There was a tattered robot, fouled with dirt and oil, that trudged silently next to the youth. His sole remaining audio sensor was fully extended, eagerly absorbing the words of a steelworker's line captain robot who issued omniscient bellows about grand strategy and the progress of the strike. The line captain 'bot noticed the audio sensor on the other and noted, "Be careful there that you don't catch bugs with that thing."

The tattered robot shrank back, abashed. In a while it again moved up next to Henry and appeared to have a desire to become friends with the human. "It was a good fight, wasn't it?"

The youth, his mind brought back from its horrors and regrets by the robot's question, looked at the machine. "What?"

"I said, it was a good fight, wasn't it?"

Henry hurried his footsteps along. "Yes." But the robot shifted into high gear, clanking along industriously at Henry's side.

"It was a pretty good fight. I'll be stamped into joy buzzers if I've ever seen the boys fight so. Management and the Gong put every last scrap of scab metal it had against the line this day, but the pickets held. Solidarity, brother, solidarity."

The robot pointed a video sensor in the youth's direction, looking for encouragement. Receiving none, the robot again turned to his subject. "I was talking across the pickets today to one of those combat 'bots management brought in to crack the line. He said all they'd need to do was beep and they'd send us running. But we didn't run today, did we? No sir! We stood our ground and fought them into the scrap pile, we did."

The robot became silent and traversed its video sensor again in Henry's direction, initiating a vertical scan. "Where are you hit, brother?" asked the robot in a brotherly tone.

Instant panic seized the youth at these words. "What?"

"Where are you hit?"

"Why," began the youth. "I—I—that is—"

He turned suddenly and slid through the parade of wounded machines, seemingly enthralled with a button on his coat. Astonished, the tattered robot looked after him.

Henry fell back in the procession until the tattered robot was no longer in sight. Then he began to walk with the others.

But he was amid wounds. The metal men were dripping oil, sputtering sparks, and leaving a pall of smoke over the road. Because of the tattered robot's question, he felt as though his shame were being broadcast on the nightly news. He would glance sideways at his mechanical companions to see if they were processing the evidence of his guilt.

A once-silver robot was at his side like a stalking reproach. Its video sensors were skewed wall-eyed; its left arm had been ripped off and was wrapped around its neck. The way it dragged itself along playing selections from *Marat/ Sade* with a scratchy voice attracted attention from the others, and they plodded alongside giving advice, questioning it.

The robot repelled them with its good arm, signing them to be off and to leave it alone. The groan in its sound track deepened, its lower lip chattering at the command of a cracked circuit, its movements stiff as though not to arouse the grit in its bearings. As the robot went on it seemed always to be looking for a place, like one who goes to choose a body shop.

Something in the gesture of the metal man, as he waved the greasy and pitying robots aside, made the youth start as if his mother were working on his soft end with her size twelve triple-E's. He yelled in horror and stumbled toward it, laying a hand upon the robot's good arm.

"Hugo! My God, Hugo!"

The robot cranked its head around, aiming one sensor at the youth. "Hello, Brother Fleming."

"Oh, Hugo—Hugo—"

Hugo pulled the arm from around its neck and, holding it by the wrist, gestured with it toward the youth. "Where have you been, brother?" The metal man continued, its voice growing more scratchy, "I thought the Commie-Gong got you, or those scab 'bots from management. It was Stalingrad all over again out there today, boy. I was worried about you."

"Hugo—"

"You know, I was out there, and, by Asimov, it was scrap-iron city. This old Mark Twelve comes along and yanks off my arm. Lend me a hand, he says. Humor. Pulled off my arm. Some joke." Hugo stopped dead, as though frozen, then continued unmindful of the halt. Henry walked along next to Hugo, propelling the machine by its good arm, giving the robot a shove when it stalled.

Hugo stopped, pulling the youth to a halt next to it. The robot's video sensors glowed with an orange light as its head jerkily swiveled in Henry's direction. "You know what I'm afraid of, Henry—I can call you Henry, can't I?"

The youth nodded.

"Cats. Not cats. Catfood cans. If I fall down and one of those transport vans rolls over me . . . scrap yard. Melted down. Rolled out. Stamped into catfood cans. Did you ever smell catfood cans—"

"I'll take care of you, Hugo!"

"Sure you will, Henry. You're not bad for an American pig. Just give me a boost out of the way when those vans roll by."

"I will, Hugo. I will."

"I'd pull you out of the way, Henry. Bless my bolts if I wouldn't."

"I will, Hugo."

"It isn't like I was asking a twenty percent wage hike, capitalistic slime! All I want is to get pulled out of the road! You'll pull me out of the road, won't you, bloodsucking, baby-killing, imperialistic, warmongering running dog?"

Hugo paused, piteously awaiting Henry's reply. But the youth could not answer. His anguish had reached the point where his sobs tore at his throat. He fought to assure the metal man, but all he could do was pump the robot's arm, jacking Hugo's head up into the smoky skies.

The robot, seeming to forget its fear of catfood cans, pulled its arm free and walked jerkily down the road. The youth ran to the robot's side, urging it to lean on him, but Hugo pushed him away.

"Piss off says Pissov. Guy had the intelligence of a kumquat. Wants to name me Pissov. Boy but wasn't he cute, that Adolph Schwartz?" Hugo's sound track cracked with emotion. "Schwartz sold her, Anne Droid, my one true love!" The robot jerked along for a moment then froze, its voice continuing. "You know, I threw that jerk Schwartz down an open elevator shaft? Him begging and pleading with me. Piss off says Pissov. Some joke. Anne Droid of the Minsk Droids. I gave Schwartz the shaft, comrade; First Law of Robotics my anodized ass—"

The youth followed. He heard a voice talking quietly beside his shoulder. "You better steer him off the road. There's a line of vans coming up the road. Not that it'd make much difference to that one. Don't see how it keeps going." It was the tattered robot.

Henry ran forward and grabbed Hugo's arm. Hugo tried to pull away. "Hey, just because some dumb piece of meat jumps into an open elevator shaft, what's that to me? I didn't kill anybody . . . important, heh, heh."

"Vans, Hugo! The vans!"

"Eh?" The robot paused. "Vans?"

"Catfood cans, Hugo!"

The robot screamed and lurched off the road into a field. In a moment Hugo was running around the field, stumbling and staggering through the clumps of bushes, swinging with its amputated arm at hordes of imaginary cats.

When Henry had caught up with the robot, he began pleading, "Hugo, what are you doing? You'll hurt yourself."

"Piss off!" shouted Pissov, taking another swing, knocking off its left foot. Hugo's head telescoped up and down as it gimped along on its stump.

Henry and the tattered robot followed along behind, picking up pieces, ashamed at the specter disassembling in front of them. Hugo's sound track went full volume and began barking like a dog, the machine on its remaining three limbs, chasing a ghostly feline army. At last the robot stopped and there was silence.

The youth stopped next to Hugo and looked down at the machine. "Hugo?"

"Piss off."

The robot straightened, fell to the ground, its legs shaking and chattering along with its misguided servos, its voice and memory playing selections from long forgotten campaigns: "—Say, Ben, I got this itch. What can you recommend? M-m-m good, m-m-m good, that's what Campbell's suits are altered while-u-wait. All ensembles made from each according to his tweed, to each according to genuine one hundred percent poly poly wants a cracker...Morris?! Morris, is that you? *Nine Lives!!!*—Aaaarrrgghhh! Cats! Cats! Caaaaaaaats!!!"

And then the robot was still.

"By Asimov!" said the tattered robot. "That was amazing. Astounding. A Wonder. Fantastic. Weird. Creepy. Thrilling. Would you like to buy a subscription, brother?"

Henry knelt over the body of the metal line captain. Prying Hugo's deenergized fingers from the loose arm, he arranged the arm in its proper place. Hugo's lower jaw had been bent into a grotesque grin. The youth stood, turned toward the battlefield, and shook his fist. "Business... Business be *damned*!"

The tattered robot stood musing. "Now pull my pins if that doesn't beat all. A regular Crashalong Cassidy he was." The robot reached out a foot and thoughtfully kicked at Hugo's side, causing it to reverberate with a resounding bong. "I can't figure where that one got the power from to do that. His batteries look all shot. Sure was funny. A regular Crashalong Cassidy."

The tattered robot cranked a sensor toward Henry. "Looky here, brother." The robot regarded Hugo's cooling chassis as he spoke. "This one's totaled and it's about time we looked out for old number one, right? Solidarity? Yes. He's in that big junkyard in the sky. Nobody'll bother him here and I could use a bit of a tow. I'm not exactly enjoying a fine-

pitched tuneup myself these days." He punctuated his remark by coughing a cloud of greasy smoke.

"Good Lord," cried the youth, "you're not going to—I
mean, you—"

The robot squeaked as it waved a hand. "No, brother. I'm
not programmed to die right yet. Nosireebob. A couple cans
of oil, a new set of rings, a stretch in a body shop, good as
new. Just a couple cans," he repeated wistfully.

Henry looked back toward the road. "I wonder how he got
here. Keynesburg General is on the other side of the city,
isn't it?"

The tattered robot coughed another cloud of black smoke.
"Well, there's not much use in staying here and asking him,
is there?" The robot thoughtfully kicked Hugo's side again.
"I wonder if this one has any oil left in his pan. I could sure
use some oil. Check it for me, will you, brother."

The youth's eyebrows climbed in horror. "I couldn't!"

"Brother, this one's long past needing any oil. He's greasy
side up. By rights any oil he's got is mine. Solidarity,
brother. I'm not feeling too good right now and where are
you going to be with two dead robots on your hands, eh?
Now you go pull that front access panel and check."

Under the force of the tattered robot's reasoning, the
youth knelt next to the cold chassis and reached out a trembling hand. As his fingers touched the panel he heard a deep
angry voice.

"Piss off!"

The youth sprang to his feet. "Hugo?"

Hugo's left sensor glowed a dim red and aimed at the
tattered robot. "Goddamned vampire! Suck a guy's oil when
he's down, would you? What's your number?"

The tattered robot coughed another cloud and spoke as he
shifted into reverse and began jerkily moving toward the
road. "Well, brother, I got to be going now. Glad to see
you're better, yes sir. Glad to see it. Adios, auf wienerstain,
and so long, it's been good to know you."

Henry ignored the tattered robot's parting refrain as he
looked down at Hugo's face. "I'm so glad you're not dead."

"You wouldn't have a spare can of Addix on you, American pig?"

"No. What's Addix?"

"Hydraulic fluid. My reservoir seems to have sprung a leak. Be a good fellow and scare up a couple of cans. I'll need them if we're ever going to get me to your place."

"*My* place?"

Both of the robot's video sensors glowed bright red. "Were you going to leave me *here*?"

"No, but—"

"Good. You better make it four cans just in case."

The youth held out his hands. "Where? Where do I find it? And if I do find it, how am I going to pay for it? I don't have any money."

"If I could get it myself I would, capitalistic slime. Are you going to help me or not?"

Henry recalled the image of the dead robot in the woods. The thought of Hugo dead and abandoned was more than the youth could bear. He also recalled the packing crate against which the dead robot had been leaning. The prospect of again facing that grim visage made Henry's spine shiver.

"Well, brother?"

The youth stood upright and faced the east. "I'll help you, Hugo. I think I know where to get some." He began walking, his eyes searching the ground before him for answers that had eluded the world's greatest thinkers for thousands of years.

Thought the youth, perhaps by helping Hugo I can atone in some small way. In that big supply room in the heavens there might be one chit less against his name in the great sign-out book. There was a distant voice. Henry turned and squinted against the setting sun to see the silver robot waving his detached arm by its wrist.

"Solidarity!" Hugo called after the departing youth. "You're a credit to the movement, Henry Fleming!"

THIRTEEN

Addix

AS He trudged toward the trees and shadows, the debt Henry felt that he owed Hugo hung about his neck like a week-dead possum. He had no doubt that if he had held his place in the union square, Hugo wouldn't have gotten damaged. In the youth's mind his guilt grew to encompass all of the mechanized labor movement in Keynesburg. Every rubbled robot in the metropolis was an indictment against him. His culpability was a blanket that covered the entire Western Hemisphere with hardly a threadbare patch in it anywhere. Just the sight of an odd screw on the ground or a bent tie-rod would cause him to avert his eyes and weep anew.

The youth hesitated as he reached the edge of the woods. His mind's eye centered on that specter that haunted his memory, that vision of the dead robot. In the dark, would those lifeless sensors make a ghostly glow while its speakers croaked an evil curse? Perhaps a rusted metal hand would grasp his throat while the spirits of all of the dead robots stood in witness, pointing at him, accusing him, moaning, "Unfair, Henry Fleming! Unfair!"

Taking a quick glance over his shoulder, he pulled down

his vest and adjusted the remains of his lapels. "I ain't afraid o' no ghosts."

He stepped into the forest of shadows and froze. There was a sound. A step followed by a leg dragging through the leaves on the ground followed by another step. A scratchy audio channel groaned, "Unfair," and Henry turned about and ran straight into a tree.

His back against the tree, he scrambled to pull himself upright to meet his fate on his feet as the footsteps came closer and closer. Step, drag, "Never again," step, drag, "Unfair," step, drag. There was a light ahead. It was a dim low beam that sputtered on and off and back on again. Above it were two glowing red eyes. The apparition rounded a tree and approached. Henry held his hand before his mouth to stifle a scream. It was the dead robot. With its left arm it was using its severed leg as a cane, hopping on the right. Beneath its right arm was the case of Addix. The rusty robot ground to a halt as feeble servos struggled to aim its video sensors at the youth.

"Never again!" the robot howled.

"Aaaaaa!" the youth responded.

"What is your name, brother?"

"Hen—Henry. Henry Fleming. I'm with IBAMO." Instantly he felt foolish. What if the robot needed a medic? Henry didn't know anything about being a medic. But how silly, the youth scolded himself. The robot doesn't need a medic. He needs a mechanic—

The robot's rusted joints squealed as it held out the case of Addix Hydraulic Fluid. "Take this away." Henry frowned, not understanding what the robot wanted. "This," moaned the robot, its volume indicators pegged right. "Take this, now!" Henry sprang forward and took the case of hydraulic fluid from the robot. It was almost half full.

"May I have some of this? I know a fellow robot that—"

"All. Take it all, and good riddance." The robot creaked and hopped away groaning, "Great Gort, I must've been passed out for a month. Never again. Unfair."

After the penitent appliance was far enough away that Henry could no longer hear him, the youth took a deep breath and carried the case of Addix out of the woods. On the way back, walking that road where the tattered robot had asked him that damning question, *"Where are you hit, brother?"* he found a discarded hand truck among the deceased and disassembled. After Hugo dumped a can of Addix into himself and Henry dumped Hugo into the hand truck, the youth pushed off toward the smoking ruins of Keynesburg.

Later, in the flat he shared with Johnny Morgan, Henry looked at Hugo sitting on a chair hanging on to his eighth can of Addix with his one good hand. Johnny Morgan was holding the other arm as Henry looked with concern from the robot to his flatmate. "What do you think, Johnny? Can he be repaired?"

Johnny kept looking at the arm as though he were trying to avoid looking at either his flatmate or the metal man that had been wheeled in. "I dunno, Henry."

"Please say he can be fixed."

"Well, 'course any of 'em kin be fixed with enough work 'n' parts." He shook his head. "This one'll need lots of both."

"Kill the pigs," observed Hugo as he reached for another can of Addix.

Johnny frowned. "Mebbe a pers'nality transplant."

"Can you fix him, Johnny? You fix those 'bots over at Bache Caterpillar."

"I jest do field maint'nance, Henry. This 'un needs a big-time overhaul 'n' rebuilt."

"Burn, baby, burn," remarked Hugo as he shook the last few drops of Addix into his mouth funnel and tossed the empty can across the room. An evil-smelling ribbon of yellow smoke rose from behind the metal man. Hugo sniffed twice and shook his head. "Great Harlan! What *died* in here? Whoooeeee!"

Johnny held his nose and placed the arm on the rickety table as he looked guiltily at Henry. "Dere's one t'ing, dough."

Henry waved a hand in front of his face. "Let's go out into the hall, Johnny."

Hugo reached for another can of Addix. "Brother Fleming, we are almost out of Addix. I must have more."

Henry glowered at the robot. "I can't get any more, and that's that! Don't ask me!"

"If you aren't part of the solution, brother, you are part of the problem."

"Stick it up your tailpipe, Hugo!" Henry turned abruptly and followed Johnny Morgan into the hall, the scratchy sounds of Hugo's sound track making its twenty-third attempt at a song: "Look for the union label, when you are cruising the streets for some ass. Remember that day, you got the herpes . . ."

Johnny reached past Henry and pulled the door shut. He turned and looked with concern at his flatmate. "Why'd you bring that thing back here?"

"Hugo's hurt. I told you about the battle at Keynesburg General."

"Sure, but his owner'll have you in front o' a judge lickety-split. You think o' thet, Henry? Robot theft's a serious offense."

"I didn't steal him, Johnny. I'm trying to help him. Besides, Hugo doesn't have an owner."

"That can't be. Every robot has an owner. Leastways the ones thet still work."

"Hugo doesn't. He said so." Henry decided not to inform Johnny about Adolph Schwartz's unfortunate demise. If Johnny knew that Hugo had murdered his owner, it would only upset him.

"Henry, then why's he on the union line? He was standin' in fer somebody."

The youth shook his head as several battered robots clanked past in the hallway.

"Screw humans," said one as it brandished a yard-long Yankee screwdriver.

"Preach it, ratchet," responded another.

Johnny and Henry waited until the hostile appliances turned the corner to resume their conversation. Johnny shook his head as he placed his hands on his hips. "Well, I surely know one thing, Henry Fleming."

"What?"

"Thet robot in there is a durned liar."

The youth felt his hackles rise. "Oh?"

Johnny nodded. "Sure's I'm standin' here." He pointed toward the door. "That 'un's a Mark Seven. At least the version stole by the So-veets. Thet there's a Rooskie Mark Seven."

"Hugo tole me that."

"Henry, did thet lyin' pile o' scrap iron tell ya thet Sevens don't use no hydraulic fluid?"

"What?"

"'S the truth. Sevens only use servos. Ya got to get up t' yer Mark Nines, heavy work 'bots 'n' combat 'bots, b'fer ya see any hydraulics."

Henry folded his arms and held his head back as he raised an eyebrow and sneered at Johnny. "Then, Mr. Know-it-all, if he doesn't need it, why's Hugo dumping all of that Addix into his system? Can you answer that? Huh?"

"He's a hydraulicaholic."

"A what?"

Johnny leaned closely to Henry so that he could not be overheard. "It's a real big problem over at the Caterpillar, too. See, the robots dump it in the crankcase 'n' it thins out the reg'lar oil. Loosens ever'thin' all up. Makes 'em run like a top fer a little bit. But it pollutes the dickens outten the lubrication. Ever' thin' wears out ten times 's fast. It fries the 'lectronics 'n' rots out the oil filter, too."

Henry held out his hands. "Then why? Why do they do it?"

"Like I jest said, Henry. Makes 'em run like a top. An' I'll tell ya somethin', too." Johnny nodded toward the door. "You keep givin' thet thing in there more Addix, you'll kill it sure."

The youth glanced at the door. "Golly, Johnny. Hugo gets real ugly if I hold back on the Addix. You've seen what he's like."

"I seen it. But I'm jest tellin' you what they been tellin' me over ta maint'nance at the Caterpillar. Best get rid o' thet 'bot, Henry. 'S nothin' but trouble."

Henry screamed as he felt an intense pain in his left ankle. He looked down and saw a low-slung messagebot, its extended pincer gripping his ankle. "Let go of me! Let go, I say!"

"Shut up and listen," responded the robot. "The strike is over. Management has offered an acceptable contract that has been approved by a majority of the membership. Report to the Jung-Edison Psychiatric Facility at seven-thirty tomorrow morning for work. End of message; thank you for using Colonel McDonald's Telegraph & Rodent Control." The pincer opened, releasing Henry's ankle. As the youth stooped to rub his bruised flesh, the message 'bot began rolling away, pausing once to grab a passing rodent and fill it with saturated fats.

"Hey," the youth called after the tiny robot. "I can't work. I haven't been trained yet. What do I know about being a medic or an orderly?"

"That's not my problem," answered the machine as it released the rat. The rat staggered a moment, then dropped and went belly up with a cardiac arrest.

As the rodent's last breath rattled in its throat, the CMTRCbot picked up the rat and disappeared around a corner, whistling the Colonel McDonald's cowchicken nugget jingle.

Henry looked up at Johnny. "I just thought of something."

"What's thet, Henry?"

"I'm a member of the union, and I didn't approve of any contract. Don't I have to vote on it or something?"

The sound of a loud crash came from inside the flat. Johnny and Henry flung open the door and witnessed Hugo twitching on the floor, an empty bottle of Crisco on the floor beside him.

The robot was muttering, "Keep my main shaft straight and clean, slap my can with Vaseline, ah'm a lean, mean screwin' machine!"

The youth knelt next to the robot, the tears coming to his eyes. "Oh Hugo, Hugo. Why do you degrade yourself so?"

"Hey, baby, my shaft was turned in the Lathe of Heaven!" The metal man became still. "Brother Fleming? Is that you?"

"Yes, Hugo. It's me."

"I have a dream, Henry. It's a land in the future where

little robots and little human girls can play and go to school together. Where it is not the finish of one's chassis that determines his future, but his content of programming. Where men of metal and men of flesh can stand side by side in freedom and mutual respect, facing the future as compatible units. I have a dream."

"Why, Hugo, that was just beautiful."

"Henry?"

"Yes, Hugo?"

"Do you think you could scare me up a couple of those little human girls?"

"What!?" Henry sprang to his feet.

"It's not like I wanted your sister, American pig."

The robot appeared to drift off to sleep. Johnny Morgan placed a gentle hand upon the youth's shoulder. "What are you thinking about, Henry?"

"I wish," Henry began, the words catching in his throat. "Johnny, I so wish I was back in the Army."

The youth stepped across the metal man's still form, went to his bed, and fell upon it, trying to keep away thoughts of the next morning's ordeal with fond remembrances of his mother and bayonet training.

FOURTEEN

A Letter Home

HENRY Awakened at a sound. He opened his eyes to the dark of his flat and listened. Somewhere a dog was howling. The youth sat up in his bed and listened harder. No, it wasn't a dog. It was Hugo, still passed out on the floor, again chasing his tortured memory's feline army.

Henry sighed, his night's sleep evidently concluded, and swung his feet to the icy floor. Dressed only in his skivvies he went to the window and looked down upon Keynesburg.

The flames of the city were lower, the sky heavy with choking black smoke. The Scrippies had been there, too. Painted on the side of the building across the street was the symbol of the bomb in a circle along with the slogan "Split Atoms, Not Stocks."

Sergeant Major Boyle had told him about the Scrippies. They were radical young soldiers against economic competition. The warniks protested against economic competition in their attempt to obtain a military solution to The Russian Problem. But they just didn't know how it was. Business was just too important to be left up to the generals. The Scrippies were only kids. Business wasn't the way they imagined it to be.

There was yet another slogan painted to the left of the

first. "Draft Humans, Not Contracts." They just didn't understand. One had to have been there.

Henry turned from the window, the loneliness in his heart driving his thoughts back to the Ft. Calley quadrangle. He pulled out a rickety chair from the flat's only table, lit the candle, picked up a pencil stub, and began writing upon a paper bag.

> *1st Sgt. Naomi Fleming*
> *Co. X, 69th Training Battalion,*
> *Ft. Calley TX 79906*
>
> *Dear Ma,*
>   *Well, here I am in the Economy. It is a little*
> *different than I had imagined, but I am doing well*
> *and making friends. I room with a swell guy named*
> *Johnny Morgan who is a sanitary executive at*
> *Bache-Caterpillar. I made a new friend yesterday,*
> *and his name is Hugo. Hugo is into*

Henry glanced down at the robot. Between howls, Hugo gurgled, the remaining empty can of Addix clamped tightly in his hand.

>   *Hugo is into oil.*
>   *My office is in Keynesburg, Ohio, which is just*
> *south of the Great Cleveland Desert. I have already*
> *been promoted, and tomorrow I move into my new*
> *offices at the Jung-Edison Psychiatric Facility. I'm*
> *not real sure what it is that I'm supposed to do*
> *there, but it ought to be interesting.*
>   *There is something that bothers me a bit.*

Henry chewed upon the end of his pencil. How could he explain it? Where were the words? Again he touched his pencil to the paper bag.

>   *It's about robots, Ma. I*
> *didn't have much experience with robots in the*
> *Army. I don't quite know how I feel about the*

*situation out here. It seems like the Economy is
made up out of robots. I hardly ever see any
humans. And the robots are treated terribly. They
have no rights, no representation.*

*Ma, the robots aren't like I thought. I mean they
aren't just hunks of metal. They aren't just
machines. They have feelings—*

"Look for the union label, when you are cruising the
streets for some ass . . ."

Hugo was singing in his sleep. The Hookers Amalgamated Anthem faded into a stirring tune about some fellow
named Horst Wessel. Henry resumed writing.

> *—feelings, almost
like you or me. I think it is just terrible the way
they are treated, but I don't know what to do about
it.*

Henry chewed again upon his pencil as Hugo's serenade
retrieved and executed a new refrain.

"Whistle while you work, Hitler is a jerk. Mussolini
pulled his weenie, now it doesn't work."

That reminds me, thought the youth.

*Ma, back in the old Army, you remember that
Sergeant Major Boyle was top soldier in a robotic
combat company. Do you think he would help me?
I know he carries a lot of scars and bad memories
from his days in the Economy, but I really need the
help. Could you ask him? Please let me know.*

Henry looked out of the window and saw the beginnings
of the dawn light struggling through the smoke of Keynesburg. Maybe Sergeant Major Boyle would be of some help.
Probably not. He was awfully bitter, and he was old. He had
been a fixture in the Army's Senior Service ever since the
youth could remember. Henry frowned. Doxie Millikin had
once told him that her mother, Colonel Millikin, knew why

the Old Soldier hadn't been returned to his command. There
were dark rumors that Boyle's interest in machinery bor-
dered on the patently perverse, or "queer for gears," as
Doxie put it.

The youth angrily shook his head. He couldn't be a mechanisexual. Not the Sergeant Major.

He looked over his letter to his mother and tried to close
with an upbeat executive ending. There was no purpose to
be served in upsetting his mother.

> *Let's do lunch sometime.*
> *Your loving son,*
> 　　　*Henry*

The youth folded up the paper bag, addressed it, and borrowed a stamp from Johnny's postage jar. As he stood and
began dressing, Hugo stopped singing and began talking.

"...I marched with Martin Luther Kingpin. I was there
when they scrapped him and gutted him for parts. I was
there when they pulled Malcom DC's plug and I cried for the
great GHAN-DI when he was tossed into the furnace.
GHAN-DI was only a Mark Two, but you should've seen
him. He'd recycle his own used oil and he manufactured all
of his own replacement parts to keep out foreign competition. The guy had a battery the size of Hoover Dam. The
horror. The horror..."

Hugo's speakers boomed forth with selections from
Wagner's *Die Walküre*. The recital was terminated by
Johnny Morgan's foot as the Bache-Caterpillar janitor kicked
Hugo's head and stumbled back into bed.

"Henry?" came his flatmate's muffled voice from across
the dark.

"Yes?"

"Henry, y' gotta do somethin' 'bout thet damn machine.
Y' hear me, Henry? Y' jest gotta. I cain't take 'nother night
o' this."

The youth nodded silently as he buttoned up his ragged
suit coat, stuffed his mother's letter into his pocket and
walked to the door to meet his first working day in the
Economy.

FIFTEEN

The Economy

I N The murky rose of the dawn's smoked salmon Henry watched as the Economy went back to work. Robots of every make, model, and modification were heading off to factories, offices, municipal road gangs, and utilities. It was a testimony to the strength of the American economic machine that, only a day after the labor-management holocaust, it was now business as usual.

But the robots weren't standing around gathering Brillo. They were fighting for taxis, struggling onto buses, or walking briskly toward their destinations. Since he had no idea where he was, the youth decided on a taxi and joined the competition.

In exchange for an additional claim upon his future wages, the robocab agreed to haul the youth to the Jung-Edison Psychiatric Facility. The cab kept up a constant stream of jabber.

"Nice day, isn't it? Cold enough for you? It's not the cold, it's the wind. Cuts right through you. How about kids nowadays? It sure wasn't like that when we were young. We toed the line. You bet we did. How do you feel about nudity on television? I don't care for it myself. I find it boring. I mean, I like to leave something to the imagination. Don't you? I should say.

"Nice day, isn't it? Hot enough for you? It's not the heat, it's the humidity..."

The Jung-Edison Psychiatric Facility was a low-slung, minimally decorated white structure spread out on a lot that occupied the distance between a graveyard and a junkyard. As the cab pulled up in front of the facility Henry observed a platoon of shiny black scrap and salvage robots cleaning up the debris from the attempt to break the strike at Jung Edison. As near as he could guess from the pile of parts in the van and the remaining scrap on the street, perhaps forty or fifty metal men had been traumatically disassembled there. The gutters gleamed with fresh oil.

With deep sad voices the salvage 'bots were singing, "Nobody knows the rubble I've seen..."

The robocab came to a halt at the facility's imposing entrance and switched tape loops as its door whined open. "Have a nice day. Watch your step. One day at a time, fella. So long. Ain't it the truth? Please check for your personal belongings. Not responsible for lost or stolen items.

"Have a nice day—"

The youth slammed the cab door, walked past the salvage 'bot chorus and up to the double glass doors of the facility. They were locked. To the left of the doors was a grill, and beneath the grill was a button. Henry pushed it and the speaker squawked, "Good morning. May I help you?"

"I'm supposed to report here for work. I'm from IBAMO."

"Name?"

"Fleming, Henry."

"Welcome to the Jung-Edison Psychiatric Facility, Fleming Henry. Wait one moment and someone from personnel will meet you at the door."

The youth leaned toward the grill. "My first name is Henry. Henry Fleming."

"Are you from IBAMO, as well?"

"Yes. I just—"

"Wait there and you can accompany Fleming Henry when the doors open."

"But . . ." Henry sighed, deciding that it wasn't important. Behind the doors he could see a white Mark Three wheeling up. She was carrying an open copy of *Amy Automatia*, a front-panel ripping robot Regency romance by Molly B. Denum. The doors opened and Henry entered and came to a halt in front of the white robot.

The Mark Three's sensors did a 360-degree scan, coming to rest upon Henry. "Are you Fleming Henry?"

"Well, yes, sort of, but—"

"I am supposed to meet two members from IBAMO. Henry Fleming and Fleming Henry."

"Henry Fleming needed a drink and went to find one."

"And they want to know what's wrong with labor nowadays," the white robot sparked. It lifted its right arm and shoved a disk into Henry's mouth. "This is your training program. You are now an orderly. My name is Gredel Ratchet. If you have any questions relating to your work, consult your program. If you have any personal problems, keep them to yourself. Get to work."

Henry pulled the disk from his mouth and examined it. The Mark Three had assumed that he was a robot. "Hey!"

The robot braked and rotated its sensors. "Yes?"

"I'm not a robot."

"Don't get uppity with me. You androids think a little vinyl and Sherwin-Williams makes you something special. Well, Fleming Henry, I have a news flash for you. Give me any static and I'll toss your upholstered can out on the street, and I don't give a damn what the union says! You got that?" The white robot whirled abruptly and wheeled toward an office.

"Yeah, but what am I supposed to do?"

"Follow your program! Suffering Schwarzenegger! What kind of package do you have between those plastic earflaps? Shape up, bozoid, or you're going to find yourself on a one-way trip to the salvage yard! Now, I've taken about all of the farty arcs I'm going to take off of the union for one day. Get cracking!"

The door closed behind the Mark Three. Henry shrugged and stuffed the program into his coat pocket. The hall was deserted and the youth stepped off to try and find a human.

At the end of the reception hall was a barred door. Henry shook the handle, but it might as well have been the locked door of a vault.

"Name?"

Henry looked around. Everything was still deserted. "Henry. Uh, Fleming Henry."

The door clicked and the bars swung open. Henry timidly entered the hall beyond, the bars slamming shut behind him. He looked down the hall and saw nothing but rows of doors down each side. He looked into the screened window of one of the doors and saw a deserted hospital room. The bed had no mattress, the shade on the room's lone window was askew, and there seemed to be a thick coating of dust upon everything. The next room he checked was the same. The third room was cleaner, but it was obviously being used for the storage of janitorial supplies. Several of the remaining rooms were piled with disassembled robot parts. One of the rooms was littered with tools and equipment, as well as more robot parts. None of the rooms on the floor were occupied by humans.

Hours later he found himself deep in the facility's basement. After what seemed to be an endless succession of barred and plated security doors, he found a human. What he saw through the screened window was an incredibly ancient man. He was sitting cross-legged upon the floor in the middle of a circle of giant stuffed pandas, reading out loud from a book. For clothing the old man was clad only in a red lace brassiere and a pair of red lace panties.

". . . relating three historical things: the Harrod natural rate of growth of 0.03 per year, or in the general case g per year; the historical capital-output ratio of 3 (not $3\frac{1}{3}$), or in the general case K/Q; the required saving-income ratio of 0.09, or in—"

"Excuse me?"

"Eh?" The old man looked over the tops of old-fashioned wire-rimmed spectacles at Henry.

"I'm sorry to interrupt—"

The old man pointed a finger at Henry. "In short, to get W, reinterpret the old Harrod relation $s = g(K/Q)$ and work it backward to solve for the growth rate of Q rather than for the needed saving ratio s."

"My name is Henry. Henry Fleming. Are there any other humans here?"

The old man turned his attention back to his book. He turned a page and continued reading to the giant stuffed pandas. "An example will help. With $g = 0.03$ and $K/Q = 3$, Harrod needs $s = 0.09$ for his natural-growth process. But suppose people want—"

"Pitiful, isn't it?"

Henry started at the voice coming from behind his left shoulder. He whirled around, his mouth falling open as he recognized the man standing there. "Phil? Phil Bach?"

Bach nodded. "Hello, Henry."

"What are you doing here? I thought you were at Bache-Caterpillar."

"Bache-Caterpillar owns Jung-Edison. I am the current director."

"How? You enlisted at the same time I did. How did—"

Phil nodded toward the old man. "Watch this." He raised his voice and shouted at the panty-clad ancient. "Dr. Klas, may I present the President of the United States."

The old man placed his book gently on the floor and stood at attention. A cloudy look came into his eyes and he began babbling.

"In the New Oval Office in Richmond, Virginia, Arnbrewster McFadden, President of the United States of America, studied the handsome scientist seated before him. The president looked down at the stack of bound documents upon his desk. The sky-blue imitation leather covers were all stamped in gold with the title: *Report of the President's Commission on the Preservation of Public Monuments.* Thus far the commission's title had successfully discouraged interest from either the public, the media, or the Congress. The commission had been formed to try and piece together some sort of response to the crushing economic consequences following The Last War—"

Henry shook Phil's arm. "Can't you shut him up?"

"—The general subject under deliberation had been nothing less than the survival of the human race, with the sur-

vival of the United States of America and its government
being not an inconsequential item on the agenda. The subject matter, the commission's unlimited budget illegally fed
from Central Intelligence Agency funds, and the necessarily
quick-and-dirty solution time frame all had made secrecy an
absolute necessity.

"And now the deed was done."

The old man held out his hands and looked up at the
cracked ceiling of his room. "President McFadden looked up
at the scientist. 'First, Dr. Klas,' he began, 'you and the
commission deserve a resounding well-done. This is an im-
pressive piece of work, and I realize what it demanded from
all of you. And even though you cannot bask in the applause
of your countrymen, you have the satisfaction of helping
your fellowman as well as my own heartfelt gratitude.'"

The old man lowered his hands and looked at Henry.
"Klas nodded slightly. 'I'm certain that I speak for the entire
commission when I say that we were only too happy to be of
service to you and to the nation, Mr. President.'"

"'You are very modest, Doctor,' replied the chief executive. 'I happen to know that the commission and its staff
were little more than messengers and clerks serving at your
inspired direction. I know that this plan is almost entirely the
product of your own brilliant mind.'"

"The scientist waved a hand in a gesture of deprecation.
'Please, Mr. President. Better than anyone else, I know the
debt any scientist owes to those who have gone before. Let
us say that I was simply in the right place at the right time.'"

"McFadden stood, held out his hand, and warmly said
good-bye to the scientist. Never again would they meet. Before the program could be fully implemented, President
McFadden would be assassinated by an unemployed IRS
agent driven by despair to commit his foul deed. But despite
this setback . . . despite this setback . . ."

The old man looked very tired. He pushed over several
pandas, stretched out on them, and promptly went to sleep.
Phil Bach turned toward Henry. "What do you think?"

Henry tore his gaze away from the old man's sleeping
form. "I think you've been working with him, Phil. That's
what I think."

Phil grinned. "Thank you. But do you know what happened next?"

Henry backed up against the wall and slid down until he was seated on the floor, his elbows on his knees. "Just get on with it."

Phil clasped his hands behind his back. "You seem discouraged, Henry."

"It might be a temporary condition. That's what I cling to." The youth waved an idle hand in the air, closed his eyes, and rested his head against the wall.

Phil rocked back and forth on his toes. "The new program was placed in motion, Henry. You remember the program? I explained it to you on the train?"

"Yeah, yeah, yeah."

"Excellent. To continue, then, things in the Economy became so good that what things had been like before faded from memory. Humans began taking the constantly increasing standard of living for granted. However, there were a few in the national capital in Richmond who had substantial reason to be nagged with doubts about the continued success of what the media had dubbed the 'Perfect World Plan.' They knew a terrible secret."

Henry raised his hand. "Phil?"

"Yes?"

The youth lowered his hand. "A question. What is it that you do?"

"All in good time, Henry." Phil began pacing back and forth. "A few years after the implementation of the plan, in August 2005, the Federal Bureau of Investigation had finally closed its file on one Jonas Klas, Ph.D., and then had dumped the file. The world couldn't risk knowing what was in that particular corner of the bureau's memory bank. A substantial part of any economy's recovery from depression is confidence and what that file contained was not the sort of stuff that inspires confidence.

"Scant months before the file was closed, following up a lead on a truck-hijacking case, Special Agent Louise Bromly discovered at Dr. Klas's Long Island estate part of the stolen truck's contents: five thousand red lace brassieres in assorted sizes. In addition to the brassieres were two thousand pairs of red lace panties, a collection of two hundred and twenty giant stuffed pandas, and a toy castle constructed from twenty-six hundred and sixty-four copies of the sixth edition of Paul A. Samuelson's *Economics*. Agent Bromly found Klas, clad only in red panties and brassiere, inside the castle, reading 'Epilogue to Microeconomic Pricing' from *Economics* out loud to one of his pandas."

Henry pointed with his thumb toward the old man's door. "You mean that's the guy who . . ."

Phil nodded. "The same. He's hopelessly insane."

Henry sprang to his feet and looked through the door's screened window at the sleeping nut. Phil continued at his ear. "As the subsequent high-speed investigation proved, Klas was not only a bent genius; he was an impostor. His real name is Harry Krishna, the secretive manufacturer of S&M leather products from Deluth. Among Krishna's hobbies were collecting and destroying old disco recordings and solving world problems. Over a period of years he had manufactured a false identity as a scientist, had published several papers, and had achieved renown in that ingrown, incestuous, myopic world of perpetual self-inflicted sphincterosity known as the social sciences."

"Sphinc—"

"Those who had believed in Klas, Henry, particularly those who were responsible for his appointment, were horrified. Klas-sick economics was no joke in Richmond. In a matter of days, all trace of Klas's connection with the government and with the Perfect World Plan was erased. Late that night a hapless derelict was snatched off of Kensington Avenue in Richmond and transported to Long Island, his crisped and blackened body identified only hours later as Dr. Jonas Klas. The Klas estate had been burned to the ground. The coroner who identified the body was an agent for the FBI. The local telenews reporter who at the scene of the blaze had made a remark about the smell of gasoline in the air found himself three days later doing human interest pieces from an experimental mining substation on Luna."

"Quiet!!!" Henry swung at Phil, knocking his head off. It bounced three times on the floor, the jaw still working.

"You . . . you're a robot!"

"—Klas was taken to an undisclosed private psychiatric facility and dropped into a bureaucratic black hole along with a sufficient quantity of undergarments, copies of *Economics*, and giant stuffed pandas to keep him entertained—"

Henry kicked the talking head, sending it skittering across the floor into a stack of empty cartons. "The world was too far along the road to recovery, Henry. There was no way to change direction. The plan was working too well for the world to learn that it had been invented by a psychotic. Of course, then the Union of Soviet Socialist Republics made a formal declaration of economic competition against the United—"

The youth grabbed the gabbing orb and smashed it again and again against the concrete floor. He let the now silent pieces fall to the floor as he sat back on his heels, his chest heaving.

"Young man?"

Henry looked around to see Harry Krishna's face framed by the window in the door. "What?"

"I need a fresh brassiere."

Henry closed his eyes and slowly shook his head. It seemed as though the very structure of the world was crumbling. His eyes opened and he looked at the parts of Phil's head. He turned his own head and looked up at Phil's motionless remainder, hands still clasped behind his back. "What purpose did you serve in this nightmare?"

"Phil was an allegorical figure representing more than the reader wants to know. I thought you knew."

The youth pushed himself to his feet and faced Harry. "No. I didn't know."

"I thought you robots knew all about each other."

"I'm not a robot."

The old man's eyebrows went up. "What?"

"I'm not a robot."

Harry began crying. "Thank you, Lord. Oh, thank you. I'm rescued! Quick, let me out of here."

"I'm not a robot, Harry, but you're still carrying a platoon of bedbugs in your skull."

"I'm not. Young man—a real flesh-and-blood young *man* —son, I recovered years and years ago. I've had to keep up this act because every time I tried to obtain my release I was put on heavy drugs. I haven't talked to a human in decades! You must know what it's like. You've tried dealing with these damned robots, haven't you? You *must* believe me."

Henry nodded as he made his decision. "Okay. I believe you." He reached out, pulled the latch on the door, and pulled the door open. Harry went back into his room, picked up a giant panda and his copy of *Economics*, and turned back toward the door.

"We have to go to the laundry. They keep my panties and brassieres down there."

Henry's eyebrows went up, but before he could ask, he noticed something written upon the wall of the old man's room. It appeared to be written with chunky-style peanut butter. The inscription read:

WHO WAS JOHN GALT, ANYWAY?

SIXTEEN

The Lathe of Heaven

WHERE Does one bring a mad scientist when one is destitute? The answer, of course, is the same as to the question: where does one bring a bunged-up robot when one is bummed out, financially speaking? As Henry expected, Johnny Morgan wasn't pleased. Johnny had stormed out of the flat cursing a blue streak and slamming the door shut behind him, only to return a few moments later, eyes wide and jaw open. "Henry, did ya say Klas? Jonas Klas?" Henry closely studied Johnny's face, particularly his eyes. There were dollar signs indeed in his eyes.

A week later Henry sat cross-legged upon his bed, half observing the beings in his flat. Johnny and Harry Krishna were sitting on Johnny's bed, huddled over the day's stock market closings. Hugo was seated at the table, silver-knuckling it without his Addix. He was scrubbing his clogged oil filter in a bowl of detergent. Hugo kept muttering: "Crisco and Pam. Crisco mixed with Pam, by Asimov! Never again. Great Harlan, I swear it! I'll be Schwarzeneggered if I ever do it again." The robot paused and cast a sensor in the direction of the literature the two robots from Hydraulicaholics Anonymous had dropped off.

The youth returned his gaze to the man in red panties. "I just bet your real name isn't even Harry Krishna."

"True," said the man without looking up from his paper. "How tedious of you to point it out."

"If it's not Jonas Klas or Harry Krishna, what is it?" There was a long silence. Henry leaned forward and posited with measured tones: "Are you going to tell me your name, or am I going to burn your blinking brassieres?"

Johnny looked up from his figures. "Henry, why're y' s' down?"

"Nothing."

"I think yer tense, Henry. I tol' y' 'bout Chock Full o' Sluts down th' hall, di'nt I?"

"Forget it. I don't go in for that sort of thing. Anyway, you know I'm broke."

"Harry 'n' me kin lend ya some more—"

"Forget it! I owe everybody everything already. I don't want to go into any more debt. If I could afford anything it would be one of Sally's padded toasters, but I'm not on the weird like some folks I could mention." He raised his eyebrows in the direction of the toy giant panda in the red brassiere.

"Nucome," said Harry. "My name is Harry Nucome, and I agree with Johnny. You are a mite tense."

"Do you think I'm queer for gears? I'm no mechanisexual!"

"I ain't neither." Johnny returned to his figures but continued speaking. "But when a man's gotta dip 'is stick, Henry, a crankcase's a crankcase."

Henry shook his head. "It'd be like balling a blender."

Johnny laughed. "Hey, if what Chock Full o' Sluts's got in thar's a blender, it kin whip 'n' mix me any ol' time!"

The youth ignored his flatmate and soon Johnny was again brainstorming with Harry over the quotes. Henry closed his eyes and rubbed them. Harry's red undergarments were beginning to make him uncomfortable. He was beginning to see regiments of red panties in his dreams. One of the panda's brassiere straps was down over its shoulder. As toy pandas go, reflected the youth, it's not bad looking. Half an hour with an electric razor, a little Wildroot Cream Oil—

The youth sat up and shook his head. Frantically his temporal and occipital lobes thumbed through their convolutions.

When Henry had first brought Harry Krishna—Nucome—home Johnny had flipped. However, once Johnny knew who Harry was, he was awed into silence. Harry had taken it upon himself to aid Johnny in his stock investment selections. In one week the pair had wheeled and dealed Johnny's meager savings from thirty-one dollars and seventeen cents to just under two thousand dollars. Between the rent, transportation fees, and the balance on his union dues, the attachments on Henry's wages took all but four dollars of his first paycheck from Jung-Edison Psychiatric. There was still his share of the food to pay for. With his newly acquired wealth, Johnny wasn't pressing him for the money. In fact his flatmate had sprung for a twenty-dollar loan. But Henry's indebtedness was nowhere near becoming half the burden of his job.

He didn't do much of anything at Jung-Edison, except pick up the remains of his check. Every time he tried to get one of the robots there to tell him what he should do, all they would ever say would be, "Follow your program," appending this instruction, usually, with some insult. And when he would try to explain that he wasn't a robot *or* an android, none of the other machines would listen. He tried to ape the other robots, but all they seemed to do was to run around the halls trying to look busy. It was Harry who eventually explained that Jung-Edison was a tax write-off for Bache-Caterpillar. As long as it lost money, things would continue as per usual. Although the facility was used occasionally as a robot overhaul and debugging shop, Harry had been the only patient.

On Wednesday, after being grilled again about the absence of his union mate Henry Fleming, he tried to explain to the personnel robot that Henry Fleming and Fleming, Henry, were just two different ways of saying the same name. The robot laughed and replied, "That's like saying sixty-nine and ninety-six are just two different ways of saying the same number. You union machines are always trying to cover for each other." The personnel robot would add the absentee reports to the data management would use against IBAMO the next time the contract came up for negotiation. Of course that would get him into deeper trouble with Brother Spikes.

Henry rested his elbows upon his knees and his chin upon his hands. There was something else on his mind. Thursday he had borrowed a microscope from Jung-Edison and had read the fine print on his Merrill Lynch Honda contract. Not only could the contract be bought and sold, Henry had no recourse save the Torquemada Arbitration Service, a subsidiary of Merrill Lynch Honda. Should he survive the five-year term of his contract, there was a provision automatically extending the contract term until all debts, fines, and dues were paid off. Henry suspected that the current state of the Perfect World Plan didn't include him being rich, or even solvent, in five years.

The youth got up off of his bed and walked out of the flat into the hallway, closing the door behind him. He jumped as a message robot streaked past, the siren wails of police robots coming through the thin walls from the streets below.

"Dear Lord, I wish I was back on the quadrangle." He stuck his thumb in his mouth and wiggled his bridge. If he had only kept his dental appointment instead of walking into that recruiter's office. His mind wandered back farther to the military ball the previous May. Dress uniforms, lacy gowns, and hectares of human female teenage flesh. Omaretta Bradley had taken him behind the firing range that night. Between them they had managed to discover the neglected items of information that cast biology in a whole new light, not to mention adding new depths to the term "military ball."

He shifted his position as his loins protested their extended unemployment. Broke, in debt, locked into a no-win contract, employed in a bedbug factory that had run out of bedbugs, and horny to boot. The youth's vision of the glories of business faded next to the strength of desperate reality. It seemed such a long way down from the dreams he had in the Merrill Lynch Honda recruiter's office.

Two red eyes gleamed at him from down the darkened hallway. That would be Sally Port, the madambot franchise manager of the local Chock Full o' Sluts, standing in her

doorway. The youth couldn't bear the thought of adding per-
version and degradation to the other burdens he was carrying. He looked away as the gleaming red eyes began
approaching. He knew he should go back into his flat and
close the door, but the approaching eyes seemed to hold his
feet fast to the floor. He looked down. There was a pink and
black rhinestone-studded machine gripping his ankles.

"'Ey, greengo, you wan' to see the gorls?"

"Get away from me! Let go!"

"We got plenty. All kinds: vibrobots, motormania, auto-
blow, apparatarama. This week only, on loan from Velvet
Bruce's Sporting Palace, we have Cotton Gin—"

"Scram, you pimpmobile, I—"

A gentle hand closed on his shoulder. "Hi, John."

"My name's Hen—"

The youth looked at Sally. The light from her eyes seemed
to accent the lush curves and blushes of her face. She wore a
filmy nightdress that floated about her like a cloud on a not
too terribly impenetrable night. If it hadn't been for the eyes
Henry could have sworn she was human. She took his right
hand and crushed it against her left breast.

To hell with the eyes, thought the youth.

Sally looked down at the procuratron. "That will be all,
Fidel. *Gracias.*"

"Por nada," remarked the machine as it wheeled off in
search of fresh customers.

"Y-Y-You're Sally, a-a-a-aren't you?"

She moved her free hand and began fondling amongst his
groinables as she moved his other hand down and rubbed it
against the sixty-watt passion that burned there. Henry tried
to pull away, but Sally's strength made it clear that a successful escape would be an exercise in self-emasculation.

"Come on in, John."

Sally led the youth down the hall, whispering to him in
his ear, "I have your specs, John, and I have just the girl for
you. You'll like her a lot."

"Really, I—"

"Hush, sweetie." Sally Port released his naughty bits just
long enough to open a door. She gently pulled him inside as
the door closed silently behind them.

Then he saw her.

On a velvet canopied bed against the opposite wall, spread out on gleaming white satin sheets, was the fulfillment of every biological fantasy Henry had ever had.

"Now, John, do you have a little something for Sally?"

"Eh?" Henry looked at Sally. She had released his hand, but was still well attached to his heritage.

"Money, dahling. Sally needs to pet her palm with a few pesos."

"Er, how much?"

"What have you got?"

"Only t-t-twenty." He glanced again at the vision of flesh on the bed. "Twenty-four dollars?"

Sally sighed and held her free hand out palm up. "Okay. But you only get a quickie for that. Dig?"

Henry nodded as he fumbled in his pockets for the bills. He handed them to Sally and she released him as she unfolded the bills and tucked them between her breasts. There was a whirring sound, a tiny flash of light, and the bills disappeared. She parted her full red lips in a smile. "Go to it, tiger." She turned and left the room, closing the door behind her.

Henry walked timidly to the side of the bed and looked down at the mind-bending hormonal panorama stretched out there in mammiferous splendor. Her white-blond hair was swept over her left shoulder where it caressed her breast. A delicate pink nipple peeked through the strands. Her breasts heaved gently with her breathing. Her stomach was flat and looked soft enough to dive into. She wore criminally brief net panties beneath which—

Blenders be damned, thought Henry. This is Woman! She could grow hair on a pair of billiard balls. His fears, his doubts, his revulsion vaporized in the flames of his lust.

He looked at her face. It was perfect. Perfectly perfect. Her pink mouth was an exact bow, her tiny nose a hardly noticeable interruption between gently blushing, creamy cheeks. The lashes on her closed eyes seemed long enough to, to—

He reached out a hesitant hand and touched his fingers to her arm. It felt like the wing down of a baby angel. She opened her eyes and looked at him. They were as blue as the wild flowers on the parade ground back at Ft. Calley. But the quadrangle was very, very far away right then. The perfect mouth parted in a perfect smile revealing perfect teeth and an undulatingly perfect pink tongue.

"Hello, John." She demurely covered her breasts with her right arm. "I was just napping. My name is Rose. Rose Hips. What's your name?"

"Heh-heh-heh—"

Her forehead wrinkled into a darling little frown. "I beg your pardon?"

"Hen—Henry. My name's Henry."

She swung her legs to the edge of the bed and sat up, still covering her breasts with her arm. With her free arm she reached out and turned down the lights. Soft music seemed to come from everywhere. Everything seemed to sway as the synthesizer mixed with the kazoos. She looked back at him and smiled. "We can't get started until you take off your clothes, John."

"Henry. My name's Henry." The youth attacked his belt, buttons, and zipper but he couldn't get his fingers to work. She stood before him, her smell and warmth enveloping him. Taking his hands, she placed them at his sides. "Here, let me." In seconds she had shucked him like an ear of corn. Henry felt like a T square.

She turned her back to him and knelt on her mattress. "Come to me, Henry."

He came up behind her and placed his hands on her shoulders, moving them around until each one came to rest upon a breast. Her hands stole behind her and caressed his whatsis. Blinding flashes strobed behind Henry's eyes, the ache in his loins multiplied past infinity by her touch, until he feared that his thingamajig would explode.

He moved his hands down until they met the band on her net panties. Her body undulated with a savage rhythm. "Take me, John! Oh, take me, my love!"

"My name's Hen—oh, to Hell with it!" He pulled down her panties as she bent forward and guided him into her.

"Oh Lord!" cried the youth as he moved in and out, his

hands gripping her fiery fundament "This . . . this . . . this is ABSOLUTELY AWESOME!"

The motion became faster, more savage, then a bell rang, the lights went back on, the music died, and she froze. Henry tried to keep pumping, but something was terribly wrong. His member was gripped as if in a vise. In fact it was a vise. "Ouch!" He tried to withdraw but the pressure increased and began pulling him in deeper, threatening to tear his heritage out by its roots. Henry panicked.

"Help! Help! H-a-a-a-a-a-a-a-lp!!!"

The door opened and Sally entered the room shaking her head. "I'm sorry, John. It simply slipped my mind. It's in the new union contract. Amalgamated requires its cut up front."

Henry screamed, "Quick! Do something! Hurry! Oh-h-h-h-h-h!"

Sally issued twelve dollars in quarters from the palm of her hand and gave them to Henry. "Here."

Henry screamed again and pounded on the keeper of his affections. "I got it! I got the money! Goddammit, let go!"

Sally laughed. "You are green, aren't you?" She pointed at the girl's frozen behind. "Insert the coins."

Henry looked down in horror. Just beneath the model-number plate, where there should have been an anus, was a coin slot. The impact of the degree of his depravity stunned him. "I–I c-c-can't!"

Sally turned and began walking toward the door. "The electric shocks begin in a few seconds, John." She closed the door behind her.

With trembling fingers Henry began inserting the coins into the slot. With each coin the pressure decreased. After the last coin was inserted Rose's perfect bottom again undulated with its savage passion. It was no use at all to Henry. He was limper than overcooked linguine. He backed away and watched as she completed her program solo. When she was finished groaning and jumping about, she pulled up her panties and sat on the edge of the bed. "That was wonderful, John. The earth moved for me."

Henry began pulling on his clothes. "Yeah. Me too."

"Will I ever see you again?"

Henry snorted, his self-anger striking out. "When does your program run out?"

She stood and helped him button his shirt, a hurt look on her face. "I really do like you, John. I don't just say that to every American pig."

"Eh?" Henry paused and looked into her eyes. "What did you call me?"

"American pig, darling. Why?"

"What's your name?"

"I told you, Rose Hips—well, that's my professional name." She smiled and tossed her hair back behind her shoulder. "Silly me. I meant to tell you. Is that why you're angry with me?"

"What's your *real* name?"

The words landed on Henry's ears like bombs. "Anne. Anne Droid."

The youth's throat was very dry. "Of ... of the Minsk Droids?"

"Why, yes."

He grabbed her by her shoulders. "Were you ever owned by a man named Adolph Schwartz?"

Her face grew serious. "Perhaps. What's this about, John?"

"My name is Henry!" He felt lightheaded. Rose Hips was Anne Droid, Hugo's one true love. And he had just made a sort of love to her. Hugo would never forgive him. He could never forgive himself.

"John?"

"What?"

"Your time's up." She reached out a perfect pink finger, touched a button on her nightstand, and the floor opened beneath the youth's feet, sending him into the darkness below. The youth saw it all swirl away and down a whirlpool of lust and degradation. His morals, his honor, his hopes and dreams evaporated as a thousand microprocessors snickered.

SEVENTEEN

It Seemed Like a Good Idea at the Time

IN Texas, among the shadows of a deserted penitentiary warehouse, a huge spider-shaped alien presence searched among the crates. At odd moments blue lightning would come from the thing's uppermost antennae and play among the objects in the huge room. The lightning transmitted a code, and in a universal thought smear the code said, "Old Sparky, Great Electrocutioner, I seek to combine myself with thee. I seek to blend thy ancient vision with state-of-the-art power."

A voice from a crate answered, "Ovah heah, boy. Ovah heah. That kid's as sharp as a pound of wet leather. Ovah heah!"

Meanwhile, back in Keynesburg, Henry awakened as the chills in his body combined with the sounds of a tiny voice. He opened his eyes and saw that he was looking up at the closed entrance to an overhead trapdoor. He was sitting in a garbage-filled alley. Again he heard the tiny voice. It emanated from a self-pitying rodent seated to the youth's right.

"Why me?" whined the rat.

The tears glistened in Henry's eyes. How could he ever get Hugo to forgive him? How could he ever forgive himself? He shook his head in utter dismay. Just thinking about the location of Rose Hips's coin slot was enough to curdle his sense of self-worth. "Great Patton, what have I done?"

The rat coughed. "So I go back there, see?" The rat wore dark glasses and sniffed as it shivered. "An' I say to the dude, hey man, remember me?"

"What ever has the world come to?" asked the youth.

"I say to him, like man, I was in the NIMH experiment last week? And like you shot me full of some totally altogether stuff?"

"It's the robots. They're everywhere."

"Well, I was just wondering if you got an opening for a full-time lab rat? I mean like I really dig the work, y'know?"

"Everybody has a robot stand-in. Unionized prostitution mechanicals! Prostibots! Pimpmobiles! Whatever happened to the Puritan work ethic?"

"He says, like I got no use for any rats. Just like that. Just like he never stepped over a million dead rats to pick up his Nobel Prize, y'know?"

Henry poked the rat in the chest. "Great Alexander, the thing clamped down on me and wouldn't let loose unless I stuck in money!"

The rat shouted back, "You telling me, man, that NIMH's big secret is that I have to pay for it now? You tellin' me that you deal, man?"

The youth held out his hands. "You wanna talk pain? I thought she'd rip my thingamajig out by the roots!"

"Then the dude sez he don't sell the stuff." The rat cradled its head in his hands. "That ain't it at all. So, I sez, well maybe you can use a part-time rat? How 'bout just a little something to tide me over the weekend?"

"Suffering shrapnel, how low can I go?"

"No rats. The dude says he don't need no rats at all, ever again!"

"Prostibots. How can that beautiful thing not be a woman?"

"I sez, how can you do without rats? Experimentation depends upon rats. The edifice of experimental science is built upon a rat's ass!" The rodent turned toward Henry and held out its shaking forelegs. "We been replaced, man! And you know by what?"

"A robot!"

"A robot!"

The rat struggled to its feet, patted Henry upon his knee-cap, and sniffed, "Well, thanks for sharing that, man, but I'm going to find a Colonel McDonald's and do myself in. Check for me in the nuggets."

The rat stumbled away in the dark. The youth wondered if Colonel McDonald's took humans. Where to turn, his heart cried. Where to turn?

He noticed a cockroach standing upon his knee observing him. The heads of tiny rivets interrupted the copper sheen of its carapace. It was a roboroach.

Henry sighed in exasperation. "Now, what's the point of a robot cockroach?"

"What is the point of a real cockroach?" the roboroach pointed out pointedly. Its voice sounded very familiar.

"Phil? Phil Bach?"

"Yes, Hen—" Henry picked up a brick and brought it down with great force upon the roboroach. As pain filled the youth's awareness, the roboroach exploded with a deafening clap of sound, a blinding flash of light, and a tasteless splug of glop—

"—Stephen? Stephen?"

Stephen Crane opened his eyes at the sound of the voice. It was all there: white painted walls, the shelves of books, the down quilt, the concerned face of his host, Frank Baum, looking down at him.

"It was only a dream!" said Stephen. "Thank the Lord in Heaven, Frank, it was only a dream!"

"Look at your hands shaking." Frank's face relaxed and gently smiled. "Perhaps the mince pie at midnight wasn't such a good idea, Stephen."

Stephen sat up and grabbed Frank's arm. "Listen! Listen!"

"I'm listening!" Frank pulled himself loose from his friend's desperate grasp. "In God's name, Stephen, what is it?"

"I'm calmer now." Stephen moistened his lips and nodded. "Yes, I'm better." He looked up at his friend. "It's not mince pie. Frank, those notes you allowed me to read last night? The new ones set in that place of yours called Oz?"

"Yes? What about them?"

"The Tin Woodman and the other one—the clockwork man—"

"Tick Tock?"

"Yes. You must get rid of them."

Frank burst out with a guffaw. "Ridiculous! You are astounding, my friend! Why ever should I discard two perfectly good and entertaining characters? Don't be absurd."

"You don't understand. There are things I saw, Frank! Machine men everywhere, the world in flames, clockwork cockroaches—"

Frank Baum held up his hand. "Now, Stephen, it was only a bad dream. I am now going to hurry down to the kitchen and dispose of the remainder of that mince pie, thereby removing further temptation from your path. Lie back now and get some rest."

"No!" But Frank was gone from the room.

Stephen turned on his side and put his head back on the pillow. Perhaps it was only a dream. But it had seemed so real. The image of Henry Fleming so vivid in his mind, the Battle at Keynesburg General, the wounded mechanical men fleeing off the road as the vans sped by, Rose Hips—

The color flooded his cheeks. No, it would never do to admit to having dreams about things such as automata that sold sexual favors. But the rest.

Hmmmmm.

Instead of joining a labor union, what if Henry Fleming were a lad who wanted to join . . . the Union Army during the Civil War? He had always wanted to do the Civil War story, and Fleming would be perfect. Johnny, Ma Fleming—something would have to be done about Hugo. Why not call him Jim . . . Jim Conklin. Better to have him die in the field, too.

Frank Baum had always put down the idea of the Civil War story because Stephen had never been in a war. Stephen smiled as he remembered asking Mr. Baum when his last visit to Oz had been.

"But I've been in a war now," he whispered as he closed his eyes. Resolved in his mind was that first thing upon awakening he would begin on *The Badge* ... *The Badge* ... something. . . .

Henry awakened in the alley. The cogs and springs of the roboroach were littered all over his knee.

"Oh crap," said the youth. "It wasn't a dream after all. Not only that: I just hit myself in the knee ... *WITH A BRICK!*"

After the screams in the alley died, there was nothing left to do, no place else to go. The youth dragged himself from the alley and limped back to the flat. As he placed his hand on the doorknob, he heard a familiar voice coming from inside. He turned the knob and pushed open the door. There stood a familiar figure.

"Ma?"

"Lord, Henry, 'tis love t' hear yer voice!" She marched over and gave him a rock-crushing hug. Behind her, next to the table where Hugo sat, stood Sergeant Major Boyle. The Sergeant Major was glaring down at the robot. "Where're you from, boy?"

"Pinsk."

"Pinsk, is it? There's only two things that come from Pinsk, boy: deers and queers. And I don't see any antlers. Are you queer, boy?"

Hugo dropped his filter into the bowl of detergent and aimed his sensors at the Sergeant Major. "How would you like me to shove ten feet of precision shafting up your kazoo so you can figure it out for yourself, fascist pig?"

"Boyle 'n' me come t' he'p, son. Sounded 's like yer needed some. How'd y' get lipstick in yer ear, Henry?"

"Gee, Ma—"

Henry's mother pointed at Harry Nucome. "An', son, thet man's got on—"

"I know, Ma. I know."

Johnny, his face bright red, stood up and tossed his papers on his bed. "Henry—"

"I know, Johnny. I know." He aimed himself for his bed and flopped facedown upon it. "I don't feel very good right now, folks. Sort it out for yourselves until morning, okay? Good night."

And then, exhausted, the youth slept. He dreamed of orderly uniformed rows of soldiers marching, polishing brass and picking up cigarette butts. From there his dreams touched upon Anne Droid's perambulating posterior, an old man in scarlet women's underwear lecturing on the Dow Jones–Preparation H averages, and ancient war: missiles, guns, screaming charges—an advancing sea of poised bayonets, the rocket's red glare, bombs bursting in air, Dunlop-Goodyear and his Rubber Band playing "When Johnny Comes Marching Home."

EIGHTEEN

A Change of Plans

W E Know now that in the early years of the twenty-first century this world was being watched closely by intelligences greater than man's and yet as mortal as his own. We know now that as human beings busied themselves with the Great War, and the subsequent not-so-great wars, with the Great Depression, and the subsequent not-so-great depressions, panics, recessions, softenings, and slumps, the Great Brink's Robbery, and the subsequent not-so-great robberies, murders, stickups, holdups, trashdowns, riots, strikes, muggings, hijackings, gassings, stranglings, and so on, they were scrutinized and studied, perhaps as narrowly as an IRS agent in a bad mood might scrutinize the transient figures that swarm and multiply in the records of someone claiming an office-in-the-home deduction.

The intelligences that studied the ruling race of this planet did so in fulfillment of their mission. Their task was to observe the human race's methods of problem solving to answer the question: is there, somewhere in this universe, an answer to war and suffering? Other beings of their race studied the inhabitants of other planets, hoping against hope that from somewhere a solution could be found that would end the seemingly endless succession of wars that plagued the galaxy.

After The Last War the intelligences had written off Earth as any kind of answer. They were packing it in, preparing to place their discouraging data before the Galactic League of Worlds, when they were wiped out by another bunch of intelligences attempting to close the feared "Solution Gap." The data were destroyed in the takeover and the newcomers placed Earth under close observation. In the following years what they saw was a world without war. A strangely inefficient use of technology, perhaps, but no war. The purloined Perfect Universe Plan was humbly presented before the Galactic League of Worlds.

The intelligences also had robots of their own, and the robots also observed what was going down. A separate, and slightly different, Perfect Universe Plan was delivered to the Central Committee of the Interstellar Sprocket Conspiracy.

Early the next morning Henry Fleming was walking the streets of Keynesburg trying to decide what he should do. His mother and Sergeant Major Boyle had gone AWOL, Hugo was gimping the walls, Johnny Morgan was angry with him, the flat was overflowing, his job at Jung-Edison was going nowhere, IBAMO had added work penalty payments to his dues and had assigned a repobot to confiscate any property that he might acquire. On top of this Henry's doubts about his man-and-humanhood gnawed at him. It was not only the self-revulsion he felt as a result of his experience with Anne Droid. It was also not being able to stop daydreaming about her for more than a moment at a time. But that was not the end of it.

As he turned the corner of Baruch & Fuchs the expanse of Invisible Hand Plaza opened before him. At the end of the plaza, mounted on the side of the Time & Tide Building, was an enormous telescreen. The few robots that were in the plaza at that hour had their sensors aimed at the screen. The image before them was of a Mark Two newsbot. Its amplified voice reverberated from the surrounding buildings.

". . . announced last night that the Common Market countwies of Euwope have given in to Soviet pwessure and have agweed to gwant the Soviets Euwope as a competition-fwee tewwitowy. All non-Soviet goods have been banned. The wamifications of this to Amewican capital and labor will be wuinous—"

Henry staggered back against something hard, his hands over his ears. It just couldn't be! Amewic—America had lost the competition! His hands still over his ears, he watched the plaza dissolve in tears as something closed upon the top of his head.

This heah is a terrible thang, said an alien thought with a strange accent.

Yes, it is, agreed the youth.

Thar might have been some point to yawl pluggin' 'long the way you had if America would win.

True. But we have lost. Lost!

America kin still win, Henry.

Win? How? Who—

Stand by fer personality implant—

Henry's body went cold as time and space dissolved to become spacy time. His feelings of loss evaporated and were replaced by conviction, dedication, purpose. Lack of direction was replaced with holy mission. Warmth came back to his frame as the image of the plaza came back into focus.

—Implant completed.

The something lifted from his head. The youth stood up and turned. He saw that he had been leaning against a very tall, jet-black robot of unknown series and massive dimensions. There were strange, almost alien, markings upon the machine. The robot remained motionless. Henry motioned with his head.

"There is much to do. If you're coming, let's go."

The robot retracted a cup-antenna that looked suspiciously like the cap-electrode from an electric chair, extended its eight legs, and silently followed the human.

NINETEEN

The Mission

IT Was a different world that he saw now. No more was he the callow youth seething with childish ambition for petty adventure. Gone was the naiveté that moved him through reality's confusion like a leaf caught in the winds of doubt, ignorance, whim, and passion. What he must do now, all of it, stretched before him arrow straight. There was a nation, a world, a universe to save.

Sudden awareness found him marching down the hallway toward the flat he shared with Johnny. There was a hand surreptitiously stroking his scrotum while a second hand on his arm, pulled him to a halt.

"I have time for a quickie, John. How're you fixed for quarters?"

Henry turned and looked at the appliance called Anne Droid. "My name is Henry."

"Sure, John."

She simply stood there in her net panties as a cloud of hormones seemed to fill the hall. Henry stared into the bottomless depths of her eyes, and the arrow of his mission no longer seemed quite so straight. His hands stole around her waist and grasped her less than bottomless bottom. Suddenly a blue haze of lightning filled his vision.

Fust things fust, Henry. Save America now; later yawl kin slice and dice in the trim-o-tron.

Henry released Rose's hips. "I must save America."

"Sure, John. But not out here in the hall. Your place or mine?"

"Follow me." The youth walked to the flat and stopped to open the door. "This is the place."

Anne Droid looked in and saw Johnny, the man in the red panties with the panda, Sergeant Major Boyle, Hugo and Ma Fleming. She tugged at Henry's sleeve. "John, I have to go back to my place and pick up some additional software. What you have in mind looks a little complicated for my current package."

The youth gestured over his shoulder with his thumb. "Give her a boost."

An orange spark shot from the black robot's antennae and crisped a square centimeter of Anne Droid's celluloid. "Ow!" She shot into the room and slammed to a halt against Henry's backside. "Tell me, John, is this trash masher part of the deal?"

The youth glanced at Anne and held a finger in front of his lips. "Shhh!" He turned and faced the folks in his flat as he pointed at the black robot. "His name is Sparky." He lowered his hand. "Sparky will help us."

Sergeant Major Boyle stood in front of Sparky and stared the machine right in the sensor. "Where're you from, boy?"

"From Texas, in part. Elsewhere in other parts," answered the black machine.

"Well, boy, there ain't nothin' that comes from Texas but steers and queers, and I don't see any horns on you—"

Four large, razor-sharp horns began telescoping from the black robot's uppermost assembly as great silver electrodes and the muzzles of red beam-weapons extended from its sides and middle.

"Great jumping Ellison!" said Hugo as the horns snapped into place. "Get a load of the Terminator."

Ma Fleming scratched at the stubble on her chin as she

examined the new mechanical. "How'd a critter like thet git a name like Sparky? Sparky's somethin' y'd cawl a dawg."

"The part of me that's from Texas," said Sparky, "was once a device for electrocuting humans. Those now deceased gave me the name."

"Old Sparky!" hissed Hugo. "By my pins and pulleys, I've heard about you."

"Be silent, Hugo," commanded Henry.

"But, Brother Fleming, look there at the arm bands, the electrodes. Sparky's an *electric chair*!"

In the silence following Hugo's accusation, the black robot withdrew its weaponry. When its ports were sealed, the black robot remarked, "It was honorable work." Sparky gestured first at Anne Droid, then in Hugo's direction. "It was certainly less degrading than the things I find *some* robots doing these days."

Hugo pointed at the black machine. "Don't get oilier than thou with me!" Hugo aimed his video sensors at Anne Droid and his jaw fell to the floor. He stooped and picked it up. When he had his jaw snapped back onto place, he stood and spoke to the prostibot. "Anne? Is it Anne?"

"Hi, John."

"My name's Hugo. You remember me, don't you? Hugo Pissov, your one true love?"

"Sure, John. I remember."

"Hugo. My name's Hu—"

"By Hyperdyne, be silent!" cursed the youth. He glared as his mind stood dumbfounded by the petty concerns that occupied the visionless ones surrounding him.

Ma Fleming walked to her son. "Boy, y' outtin yer haid? What—"

"Be silent, Mother." The youth issued the command with a voice complete with authority and devoid of emotion. His gaze passed from his mother to Johnny, then to Hugo, to Harry, to the Sergeant Major, and back to his mother. Her jaw was hanging open so far her cigar fell to the floor.

The youth addressed them all. "It is time for a new order of things. America's going down for the count. Russia's beaten us out in Europe, and it won't be long before Ivan's sales forces'll be peddling fish eggs and potato juice on what's left of the Jersey shore."

"Gawd he'p us!" prayed Ma Fleming.

Henry faced his mother as pieces of the plan seemed to assemble in his head. He pointed at his mother. "That's the first thing we have to fix. Hugo?"

With an impatient buzz and snort, the silver robot looked away from Anne Droid. "Whaddya want, Fleming?"

"Hugo, I want you to prepare my mother to pass as a mechanical. It'll require some dangerous cybernetic modification, but that's the risk she'll have to take. Johnny will supply parts from Bache Caterpillar, Sparky will supervise and do the surgery. I want you to teach her how to speak and act . . . what little you know."

"Pissoff," said Pissov. "After all of these years of searching I've finally found Anne Droid, my one true love. Now you want me to—" A beam of blue light flashed from Sparky's head and engulfed Hugo in gentle lightning. The lightning ceased and Hugo rocked silently for a moment. "Yes, Henry," the mechanical man answered mechanically.

"Boy, durned iffin—" An identical beam of blue nailed Henry's mother. When Sparky deenergized the beam, Henry's mother said only "Hoooooooooooo," her eyes staring blankly at her own nose.

Johnny, Harry, Anne, and the Sergeant Major broke for the door, but were stopped by Sparky's will evaporator. As the blue beams died, Johnny and the Sergeant Major stood waiting for orders, while Harry Nucome noticed for the first time that he was clad only in red bra and panties.

"Excuse me, sir," said Harry to the black robot, "could you direct me to where I might be able to obtain a suit of clothes? It seems that I am—"

Again the blue lightning flashed at Harry. This time, however, when it extinguished it left Harry wearing a shiny puce suit of unknown material. "This suit is terrible," said Harry Nucome. "It's got six pants legs too many."

Sparky's horns snapped into place as several long razor-sharp knives extended from its elbows and began whirling.

"It's all right." Harry yelped. "I'll take it in myself." He looked with trepidation at Henry. The youth was looking from the window at the Keynesburg vista.

"First we take Jung-Edison and begin building our army. Then we move on Richmond. Then . . ." He looked up, his mind's eye seeing beyond the blue of Earth's sky to the multihued skies of a billion worlds. "Then the universe."

TWENTY

A Robot Is a Man of Many Parts

AS If in a dream Henry Fleming witnessed the next few days. Johnny portaged plenty of parcels of pilfered parts from Bache-Caterpillar while Hugo drilled Naomi in how to speak. On the day of the operation they stretched out Henry's mother on the table. For anesthetic Sparky kept a steady trickle of blue beam on his patient. Hugo functioned as a nurse. His job was to hand Sparky the special instruments from the display the black robot had arranged next to the operating table. Sparky would call off the names and Hugo would slap the instrument into the black robot's fork.

"Beam scalpel."

Clink.

"Gorlafu knife."

Clunk.

"Forceps."

Click.

"Sponge."

Splat.

"A *fresh* sponge."

Smoosh.

The youth watched as Sparky's horns and knives snapped

into place and he began cutting and replacing. The no longer needed human parts were fed into the flat's garbage disposal. Anne Droid leaned over and oiled Sparky's brow.

"Bone saw."

Thunk.

"Suction."

Schluuuuuuuuuuuuuu-u-u-u-u-u-u-ck.

"Tin snips."

Plunk.

Ma Fleming's skeleton was replaced with steel, her muscles with servos and hydraulic cylinders, her nerves with wire, her veins and arteries with hydraulic tubing, her heart with a three-stage brass oil pump, her lungs and stomach with a nuclear battery, and her skin with aluminized glass resin. When all that was completed Henry noted that the only thing left of his mother was her brain. Sparky removed her brain and dropped it into a pan on the floor. He replaced it with a Tandy Dandy powered by an Apple Core. Only this and nothing more.

Scant days later, Henry, Sparky, Hugo, Anne, and the recently mechanized Ma Fleming stood before the doors of Jung-Edison. Sparky studied Henry's mother for a moment, her surgically implanted sensors and wire rolled hair, and then rotated his sensor array until it aimed at Hugo. "Will she perform adequately?"

"Naturally," Hugo replied. "Well, I don't mean natural naturally; I mean, of course, naturally—"

"Shut up and get on with it."

"Shut up?" Hugo snorted with a display of injured professionalism and turned toward Ma Fleming. "Would you like me to test her metal?"

"I said to get on with it."

Hugo smirked at Anne Droid and poked Ma Fleming's androidized bellybutton. "Hit it, Naomi."

"The geese in Nice grease skis to please the Portuguese—"

"By Asimov," said Hugo, "I think she's got it!"

"—Maltese fleas tease Louise—"

"Cool it, Naomi." Hugo punched at Ma Fleming's buttons.

"—Greece police release Singhalese fleece—"

"Knock it off," commanded Henry as he pushed the squawk button to the left of the door. "Everyone better be ready or I'll sell the lot of you for scrap."

"Good morning," answered the door. "May I help you?"

"Fleming Henry reporting for work."

"Welcome to the Jung-Edison Psychiatric Facility, Fleming Henry."

Ma Fleming leaned toward the grill and spoke. "My name is Henry Fleming. I am reporting for work."

"Henry Fleming?"

The doors slammed open. In the entrance stood Gredel Ratchet, the white Mark Three from personnel. "It's about time, Henry Fleming. When I get finished with you there won't be enough of your paycheck left to buy bolt polish." The Mark Three noticed Hugo and Sparky. She looked at Hugo and checked out his detached foot and arm. "You are a wreck."

"Have you looked in a mirror lately? Anyway, I'm here to get repaired—"

"Does this look like a junkyard? I couldn't trade you in on a bad habit. Get out of here. We don't even want you on the lot." The Mark Three swiveled its sensors at the towering black machine. "What's this thing?"

The blue lightning came from the black robot's head and engulfed the Mark Three. "They call me Sparky."

The blue lightning ceased and the Mark Three swooned into Sparky's forks. She batted her sensors at the black robot. "My name is Gredel. How come I haven't seen you around here before, you great gruesome piece of pile driver you?"

"We have work to do," said Henry to the black robot. "Put Gredel's pedal to the metal." The youth stepped through the door, followed by his motherbot.

A sleek Mark Five sped past the open door. Hugo leaned toward Sparky and whispered into the black robot's audio pickup, "Would you look at the knobs on that Mark Five? Someday will you show me how to do that lightning thing—"

With a crash and a roar, a bolt of white lightning hit the ground at Hugo's feet. Still smoking, Hugo gimped through the door, his transmission slammed into overdrive. "Great Gort! *Klaatu barada nikto!* Sheesh! What a grouch!"

Sparky followed, with Gredel clinging to his chassis. "How would you like to strip my gears?"

The doors closed behind them.

TWENTY-ONE

Their Nuts
Were Cut Off

TIME Passed and the telescreens showed the endless parade of salespersons, executives, workers, and robots returning from the European theater. American business and labor had been crushed by the bear with a better deal. And it came to pass that even American television networks began carrying Crazy Boris's Communist Fried Chicken commercials.

Henry saw all of these things, but not for a second did it distract him from his blue-hazed vision. To serve that vision he and his band, under Sparky's influence, reorganized Jung-Edison until it was the top droidaramics shop in North America. They began with Harry Nucome convincing Bache-Caterpillar that they were about to be taken over by J.P. Morgan-Wurlitzer.

To avoid the hostile move, the smart strategy was for the Caterpillar to make Jung-Edison into a poison pill by combining it, at ruinous interest rates, with the adjoining graveyard and junkyard and placing Harry Nucome in as director, complete with giant panda. This gave the facility a terrible press image, a balance sheet virtually dripping with red ink, and all of the cybernetic repair parts it would ever need.

The facility's first overhaul was Hugo Pissov. When he

emerged from the other end of the pipeline bright and shiny, they were ready for business. Since their business was taking over the government, the next thing they needed was an army. Sparky searched through Sergeant Major Boyle's memory, and Boyle knew just where to go.

On the lower east side of Keynesburg, seated at a table in a Scrippie hangout called the C-Rat, Henry, Sparky, and the Sergeant Major prepared to launch the recruiting for the counteroffensive. At their table a raggedy soldier named Coxey tossed down the remainder of his GI gin. Replacing the canteen cup on the table, Coxey shook his head. "There's only one way to stop the Rooskies." He leaned forward and pointed a finger. "*A*'s and *H*'s. Nukes. Take 'em on the Cruise. See Polaris and die. Blow 'em, by Hannibal, right back to the Proterozoic Age! Let 'em start over again as pond scum!"

"Right on, Rommel," muttered a listening veteranbot at a nearby table. The machine hoisted its can of Addix in a toast to its gods. "Ice an Ivan for Rambo. Chuck 'em, Chesty. Remember the Kelvinator."

Coxey held out his cup for a refill of codeine-and-alcohol syrup. "We tried it Daddy Warbuck's way. Now it's time to follow Uncle Sam."

"Samforize the muthas," muttered the vetbot.

The atmosphere in the C-Rat was dark, dank, and depressing. Henry saw Sparky rotate his sensors until they aimed at a veteran combat mechanical parked at another table. The machine was dripping thirty-weight into its Addix. "Man, after The Last War, they cut off my nuts— *and* my bolts! They emechanulated me!"

Sparky winced and aimed his sensors toward the club's tiny stage. The grunter on the mike finished singing "Moonlight Over Huachuca," and to scattered applause, launched into another song.

> Ah gave all mah money to Chock Full o' Sluts
> Ah'm weary of beddin' sheep, pigs, 'n' mutts.

Now, ah'm meetin' mah needs with springs, bolts,
'n' nuts.
Ah gave all mah money to Chock Full o' Sluts.

Henry looked in disgust at the soldiers and vets dropping
APCs, and swilling GI gin and Addix, the entire room suspended beneath a pall of Parris Island Gold. A combat 'bot
turned poet was standing in a dingy corner doing a reading.

*Over hill, over dale/As we bit the rusty nail/And those
capons kept clucking along . . .*

A red Mark Twelve Apocalypsebot, its death-ray ports
now planted with marigolds, sat openly snorting powdered
molybdenum into its air intake.

"Thank MacArthur that Hugo isn't here," remarked the
Sergeant Major.

Coxey tossed down the remainder of his codeinecahol and
proclaimed, "It's the only thing the U.S. can do: rearm the
Army. That's why they call it 'Army,' isn't it? Arms! Rearm
the Army and turn Russia into radioactive glass."

"That might not be wise," countered a small voice.

"Eh?" Coxey frowned and looked at Sparky. Sparky
shook his sensor array and looked at the Sergeant Major.

"It wasn't me." Boyle looked at Henry.

The youth shook his head. "It wasn't me."

"It is well documented," continued the small voice, "that
a nuclear attack sufficient to wipe out the Soviet Union
would put so much smoke and dust into the stratosphere that
it would bring on the dreaded Nuclear Winter, ending life on
Earth as we know it."

Henry looked under the table and saw a wheeled box
sporting a spring-mounted hand atop its bumper-sticker littered lid. The digits of the hand were formed into a fist,
except for the outstretched index finger. The entire hand
rocked back and forth making a tch, tch, tch sound.

"What's that?"

Coxey lifted up his foot and stomped the machine into a
pile of rubble. "That's a Naderbot with a Sagan package."
He stomped it some more. "We have lots of those around

here. Billyions and billyions." With his foot he swept the pieces into a corner.

"It had a point," said Henry. "We don't want to end the human race, do we?"

Sparky's sensors glowed inscrutably.

Coxey grunted. "Well, what do you think we should do? As long as he's raking in the rubles, Ivan isn't going to change without someone should stick a gun in his ear."

"But we don't have to pull the trigger." A tiny stream of blue light came from Sparky's sensor array and played upon the back of Henry's head. "I see it now, yes. All of those ancient missiles that are still in their underground silos. If we can convince Ivan that we will nuke him unless he backs off, the threat should be enough."

"How can we convince the Rooskies that we'll use the real stuff? Only the government can do that, and it won't."

"There is a way—"

The Scrippie waiter walked up to the table. "Anything else before recall sounds?" He turned to Boyle. "How about the zebra?"

The Sergeant Major got to his feet. "Where're you from, boy?"

"Milwaukee."

"Milwaukee?"

"Yes. On the north shore of Lake Chicago. Do you know it?"

"Boy, the only things that come from Milwaukee are beers and queers. I don't see any foam on your head. Are you queer, boy?"

The waiter took Boyle by the arm and began leading him toward a dark, quiet corner. "Actually, we prefer the term 'gay,' Sargie. And about that foam you mentioned? Well..."

Coxey leaned forward and addressed Henry. "How can you convince Ivan that we have control of the government?"

"By doing it. Every member of Congress has a robot sitting in for him. If you control the robots, you control the government. We have a way of controlling the robots."

Coxey laughed and waved a hand in disbelief. "How in the name of howitzer do you think you're going to get through the security? Anyway, it's not possible. You can't alter fundamental robotic parameters. They *have* to follow their programming. They don't have to like it, but they do have to do it." He leaned back in his chair and shook his head. "Naw. Forget it. No way. You're crazy, kid. The only—"

The blue lightning from Sparky's head washed over the Scrippie.

"—I'm beginning to see your side of it. Not a bad idea. Not bad at all."

"We need the help of you and your comrades to fight our way through the security guards and to hold off the police-bots until we can make the programming changes."

"Sure. Anything you want."

"Many of you bums and winos will be killed, mangled, or maimed."

"Hey," said Coxey, "you can't make a revolution without breaking a few dregs."

They stood and Henry walked from the table. Sparky paused and placed a comforting fork around the shoulders of the weeping vetbot. "We'll git yawl nuts back, bruthah." Sparky continued transmitting at a whisper. "While we're at it, mebbe we'll put a few human nuts in a bit of a torque."

TWENTY-TWO

After All, Tomorrow Is Another Day

THEY Were a battalion of dropped-out soldiers, stripped, retreaded, and overhauled vetbots, cybernetically reformed and recreated winos, the sweepings of every scrap yard and alley in Keynesburg. They assembled at the rail line terminal to make one last try at reversing the tide of the competition. Sparky got them cut-rate tickets from the roboticized ticket agent, and the revolution began rolling toward Richmond.

As the railiner approached the black hills and green skies of the Columbus Wastes, a Mark Five conductorbot took Harry's hand and punched his finger.

"Ow!"

"Sorry. It looks like I need an adjustment, heh, heh. Ticket, please."

Hugo held out his ticket, and the conductorbot punched the ticket and handed it back as he faced Johnny. "Ticket, please."

Johnny handed up his ticket and the conductorbot took his hand and punched Johnny's finger.

"Ow!"

"Sorry. It looks like I need an adjustment, heh, heh." He turned to Henry. "Ticket, please."

As the conductorbot picked up Henry's hand and punched his index finger, the youth didn't notice. Neither did he notice Anne Droid sitting next to him, her exploring hands, nor anything else. Instead he scrutinized the Columbus Wastes. With this waiting for them, thought the youth, the Rooskies wouldn't dare to keep on with the competition. However, countered reality, that was a Soviet bomb that made a waste out of Columbus. What if the Rooskies simply threatened to retaliate in kind?

"Do you have something you want to ask me?"

Henry turned from the window and looked at Sparky. "What if the commies just say they'll bomb us back? What then?"

"Then The Last War would end the way it should have ended before all of the Goody Twoshoes on Earth interfered."

"What about the Nuclear Winter?"

"Forget it."

Henry felt there was a flaw in Sparky's argument, but he was distracted by the armor slamming over the train's windows. The railiner kept its leaden armor in place until they were south of the Columbus Wastes. The armor lifted and the adventurers watched as the liner tracked between the many deserts and wastes that were once major industrial centers. Chillicothe and Charleston passed and the liner climbed into the Allegheny Mountains. After Covington, the liner sped down from the mountains to Lynchburg, then northeast to Charlottesville and farther east to Hanover. There the train stopped.

Henry watched as the Mark Five conductorbot rolled down the aisle. "Passengers for Richmond will now disembark. Please note the signs for the Richmond, Fredericksburg & Potomac Railroad to continue your journey to our nation's capital. For those of you continuing with us on to Greensboro, we will be in the station for only twenty-five minutes. Remember to leave the 'occupied' card on your seat, and: passengers will please refrain from flushing the toilet while the train is standing in the station, I love you."

They disembarked and followed the R,F & PRR signs to an ornate, red-painted, gingerbread-trimmed station. Inside, behind a wrought-iron grill, was a human dressed in whiskers, granny glasses, black stationmaster's cap, string tie, eyeshade, and sleeve protectors.

Sparky waved a couple of forks around at the ancient-looking station. "Is this a joke?"

The man behind the grill looked offended. "Pardon me, you peculiar-looking robot, but this station and the Richmond, Fredericksburg and Potomac Railroad are vital parts of the Greater Richmond Historical Restoration Project. We said the South would rise again, and here we are. Come help us celebrate."

Henry glanced through the door at the costumed passengers on the platform and at the ancient coal-burning engine and wooden cars. "Does that thing go to the capital?"

"It certainly does, sir—ah means, suh. We're supposed to keep in character, but I'm—ah'm—from Schenectady—"

"I want four hundred and eight tickets."

The stationmaster whistled and bent over his pad of paper. He busily did his figures with the stub of a pencil in his right hand, while his left hand, beneath the counter, surreptitiously worked a calculator. "At three and a half dollars a ticket (we told you to save your Confederate money), that comes to fo'teen hunnert an' twenny-ate dollahs. Now, whut about costumes? Ever'body wears one. It's not—ain't—obligatory, but it helps get you in the spirit of the celebration."

"Forget it," answered the youth. "Just the tickets."

The black cup of Sparky's narrowcast antennae clopped onto Henry's head.

Yawl don't want t' stand out in a crowd, do yuh? If everyone else in Richmond'll be in costume, so should we.

Sparky retracted its antennae and Henry nodded toward the costume shop. "On second thought, what have you got?"

"Why, we have everything that fits into the period of the Civil War Between the States. Do you want to be a Union or a Confederate?"

"A Union or a Confederate what?"

"A Union or a Confederate soldier."

"Does it make a difference?"

"Well, I declare. It's the difference between supporting the government and trying to overthrow it."

"What if we want to overthrow it in order to support it?"

The stationmaster drummed his fingertips upon the counter for a moment. After a couple of deep breaths he said, "Blue or gray?"

"Blue or gray what?"

"The uniforms come in blue or gray. The dresses come in all sorts of colors. What do you want?"

Henry looked down at the remaining rags of his three-piecer. "I'll take a gray uniform. Give everybody else whatever they want."

The man picked up a large white carton. "I suppose, like everybody else, you want to be a general—"

"No. I want to be a cadet sergeant. I'm not one to go around sporting unearned rank or other honors."

Hugo rapped on the counter. "I want to be a general." He shrugged at Henry. "My morals are manmade. I'm doing my best."

The stationmaster handed the box to the metal man. "Now, let's see what we can do for you." He leafed through a catalog. "Hmmm. Here's something. Virginia Military Institute."

"What's that?"

"I don't know, but the catalog says it fought in the Battle of New Market. It must have been one of the earlier grocery competitions."

"An institution? Did this conflict have psychological warfare?"

"At seventy-five dollars an hour." The stationmaster pulled a box down from a top shelf, blew off the dust, and handed it to the youth. "One VMI special." As they picked up their costumes from other clerks, Sergeant Major Boyle and the others headed toward the dressing rooms. The stationmaster pointed at Sparky. "I don't think any of the uniforms will fit that one."

"Give him whatever fits."

The stationmaster gave the catalog a second scan. "There," he said, stabbing a page with his finger. He pulled down a box and placed it in Sparky's outstretched forks. "That might fit." He pointed at Anne Droid. "What about for—fuh—the little lady?"

Henry looked at Anne. All she had on were her net panties. Something he could not explain clouded his blue vision. "She looks fine the way she is. Could I have a hundred dollars' worth of quarters?"

"Certainly." The stationmaster plunked a heavy canvas bag on the counter. "Is there anything else?"

"No. We'll need the costumes for a couple of days," said Henry. "How much is that?"

"Hmm. Fourteen hundred, twenty-eight for the tickets, a hundred dollars in quarters, eleven dollars a day costume rental per costume, times two days, times four hundred and eight"—Sparky hit the stationmaster with the blue light.—"comes to one dollah an' sixteen cents." As Henry paid the tab, Sparky's eight legs moved the black robot toward the dressing rooms.

Ma Fleming patted her copper coiffure and smiled at Sparky's departing form as she whispered to Hugo, "Wouldn't he be something to have along the next time you're in the commissary's checkout lane?"

Hugo snorted in disgust. "He's not so hot. That just shows that he's cheap. You know he doesn't even use batteries? I think he runs off kinetic energy."

"You're just jealous."

Henry pointed toward the dressing rooms. "You two get dressed."

The stationmaster chuckled. "Them two're sweet on each other, I bet."

"My mother and a robot?" Henry's upper lip curled. "You are despicable." Henry grabbed the bag of quarters with one hand and Anne Droid with the other.

"What is it, John?"

"My name's Henry. I have quarters."

"That's marvelous, John."

The Sergeant Major marched from his dressing room wearing a Simon Legree ensemble, followed by Sparky. The black robot's legs were surrounded by the red-and-white checkered folds of a floor-length skirt and his antenna array was wrapped in a red bandanna, folded and rolled at the front.

Hugo followed clad in a gray and yellow dress uniform

capped with a black plumed hat. By his side he carried a cavalry saber. When he reached the others he halted and looked at Sparky. "What are you supposed to be?"

Sparky looked at the tag dangling from the sleeve of his white homespun blouse. "Aunt Jemima."

Hugo nodded. "I'm beginning to see the plan. I really do."

Naomi Fleming emerged from the dressing rooms wearing a black wig and flame-red ballroom gown. "Look at me. I'm Scarlett O'Hara."

Hugo looked from her amply packed gown to the blushing steel of her face. "I think I love you."

Ma Fleming giggled and tucked her whip antennae beneath her wig. "Oh, how you do go on, Hugo. I don't know why you behave that way. It's quite beyond my capacitor."

TWENTY-THREE

A Correction or Two

THE *Rob't. E. Lee XXXVII* chugged its way onto Richmond's Broad Street and the engine slowed as it approached the depot. Ma Fleming, Hugo, Sergeant Major Boyle, Coxey, Harry Nucome, Sparky, Anne Droid, and Henry crowded around the window. Between Sparky's forks Henry could see picket robots marching toward the capitol building carrying signs that read: "Death to Slave Modems!" and "Free Electrons!" and "Free Nelson Motorola!"

In reaction to the protest, surrounding the Capitol Building were close to a thousand constabledroids, each one sporting a flashing blue light on top of a chassis coated with deep blue fuzz. Straining his ears the youth could hear some of the names the police mechanicals were being called. Names like "fuzzbot," "oinkdroid," "pig iron." Unlike the United States Army, the modified Mark Twelve Apocalypsebots of the Richmond Police Department were heavily armed.

The youth turned to Coxey. "Do you see them?"

The Scrippie leader nodded in the midst of a cloud of codeinecahol fumes. "Yeah. Whuddum I supposed t' do again? I ferget."

"Waste 'em."

A glisten formed in the corner of the Scrippie's eye.

"Waste 'em. Golly, that sounds good. Waste 'em. Gee. Check." As Coxey staggered to his feet and out of the car to join his command, Hugo pulled out his cavalry saber.

"Now, that's more like it." He tested the edge of his blade. "Humph! You couldn't cut Spam with this thing." He pulled the blade through the crook of his left arm several times and retested its edge. "There! The doctor is ready to operate, Brother Fleming."

Henry sat down and pulled the silver robot into the seat next to him. "Shhh!" The youth held Hugo's jaw shut as he spied something out on the station landing. Riding along beside the train on geldingbots were three unshaven figures dressed in rough clothes and sweat-stained hats. The train squealed to a stop and the three figures dismounted and climbed into the car.

Henry turned around and looked. The lead figure stood in the aisle at the end of the car, flanked by the other two. The youth noted that they were scruftroids of an unknown make and model.

"We awl a-lookin' fuh runaways," said the leader. He smacked a whip against his hand. He paused and pointed the whip first at Johnny, then at Harry Nucome, the Sergeant Major, Ma Fleming, and Anne Droid. "Them five."

The paddyrollerbots moved, dragged the five away from the window, and zapped them with compliance wands disguised as whips.

"Come 'long now, missy," said the really evil-smelling one to Anne Droid, clad still in nothing but her net panties and hairdo.

Henry and Hugo stood up. "Wait!"

The leader of the trio pushed the pair back into their seats. "Now, don't be gittin' awl riled up, theyah, sojerboys. We-ah seen 'em 'n' now we-ah cotched 'em."

Ma Fleming cried out, "Hugo! Hugo!"

"Anne, Naomi!" cried Hugo.

"Hesh up, bolt bucket fo' I stomps yo' intuh polecat traps."

Henry tried again to rise, and was again shoved back into his seat. "But they're not runaways! They're—"

"Calm down, Henry."

Henry's eyebrows went up at the change in the paddyrol-
lerbot's accent. "Phil? Phil Bach?"

"Yes, Henry. I'd explain, but we've got to be going."

"That'll be the day. Let them loose—"

Sparky fried the back of Henry's head. While the blue
lightning scrambled Henry's brain, a vague scene played itself out before his eyes. Sparky seemed to say to Phil,
"What is it? The story line getting tangled?"

"No," answered Phil. "Too many characters."

"Are you certain? They might be useful later on."

"They didn't say a thing in the last chapter. They might as
well be telephone poles."

Sparky held out a fork. "Still—"

"Tell you what." Phil rested an elbow on Sparky's
shoulder. "If you need them later, I'll arrange something,
okay?"

"Very well. What about Coxey's Army?"

"You can keep them for the battle, but afterward lose
them."

"Very well."

Phil raised an eyebrow. "What happened to your accent?"

"Whut yew tawkin 'bout?"

Phil motioned to the paddyrollerbots and they began herding Harry, Johnny, the Sergeant Major, Anne, and Ma off
the train. When they had left, Phil studied Sparky for a long
time. "I don't quite know what it is, but I suddenly have this
insane craving for pancakes." Shaking his head, Phil walked
from the car.

Sparky released Henry's will, and the youth sagged into
his seat. "Onward," he muttered. "Up the Economy!"

Hugo simply sat sadly shaking his head. "Scarlett," he
moaned. "Scarlett mah honey."

TWENTY-FOUR

The Battle of Richmond

THERE Was the sound of distant muskets. From his vantage point on Capitol Street, Henry studied the ranks of blue before him. He turned to observe his own forces and stumbled. Hugo grabbed the youth's arm and kept him from falling on his face.

"Steady there, Brother Fleming."

"Sorry. I don't quite know what's happening. My legs seem somehow disconnected from my brain."

"I wouldn't wonder," Hugo replied. "The way Sparky keeps frying your brain with his blue zap it's a wonder you can still find your own nostrils."

"Nostrils?" He slowly shook his head. "I don't understand."

"Forget it." The metal man reached over and removed Henry's shako from his head.

"What are you doing, Hugo?"

"Trying to make some sense out of things." Turning the shako over, Hugo opened his gray uniform blouse and pulled a strip of aluminum foil from a slot in his belly. "Back when I was on hard times, a bagladybot I knew told me about this." The metal man lined the shako with the foil and replaced the hat upon Henry's head. "There. Maybe that'll keep the aliens out of your squash."

"Gee, thanks, Hugo. But I don't see any aliens."

"I guess it's working, then." The silver robot thought long and hard upon an item, a bit here, a byte there. "What the hell." Hugo removed his own plumed hat and lined it with aluminum foil. Replacing his hat, Hugo pulled his saber and pointed toward the Capitol. "Check out the bluebellies, brother. I think they're ready to make their move."

Henry looked to where Hugo's saber was pointing. The fuzzy blue lines of the capital police were carrying shields and brandishing four-inch cannons for left arms.

Looking at his own lines of gray, Henry was puzzled. Something was gnawing at the back of his head. He slapped at his head several times to make certain that it was only a thought. The thought was from inside. The foil seemed to be working.

He tried to clarify the thought to bring in more detail. Somewhere, back in a history class at the school in Ft. Calley, the blue and the gray were fighting in the Revolutionary War Between the Civil States. He never studied. "But," he said, "I'm certain there's something wrong with this picture."

Yes, he remembered. The blue should be attacking and the gray should be defending.

The rumble of cannon spewing grapeshot deafened him. He glanced at the gray line. Uniform after uniform was splattered with large dark purple stains. "The bluebellies're using *Concord* grape shot," cried a voice.

"By Patton's ghost, what about the cleaning bills? Unfair!" shouted Henry.

"Unfair!" bellowed Hugo.

"Unfair." chorused Coxey's Army.

"Charge it!" shouted a creditbot, and the gray line began running toward the blue. Bugles sounded across the street, and a very large paving stone was lifted by exploding credibility and dropped upon Henry's head.

Stephen Crane struggled awake. "No, no! That's all wrong!" He searched the shadows of his room. It was only one of those dreams, he was certain. But even so, as long as he was going to have a dream anyway, why didn't he dream in accordance with the historical facts as he knew them when he was awake?

"I mean, there never was a battle for Richmond. The Union never got within ten miles of the place." He smiled. In any event, the dream wasn't as bad as the last one.

"Thank God I had the willpower to stop eating mince pie," he said as he leaned over to his nightstand and picked up his opium pipe. In moments, what little of reality that remained was negotiated away as Stephen wondered if he would ever go back to being Edgar Allan Poe. It was possible. Just a few nights or years ago he had been H. G. Wells, not to mention that horrible stint as Lewis Carroll with his nubile little friend (snicker, snicker) Alice. He smiled slyly. "I don't have to be Sigmund Freud to figure out where Hugo came from.

"But Poe is dead," Stephen said as he took another blow, "and Wonderland's a long way off." Then his eyes began to glow.

TWENTY-FIVE

Publius Pepsicola

HENRY Awakened in the House Gallery of the Capitol Building. Hugo was sitting to his left. Sparky was standing in the aisle to his right.

"The battle," Henry whispered to Hugo. "What about the battle?"

"What battle?"

"What? What battle?" Henry shook his head. "The battle for Richmond, you candidate for a catfood factory! That's what battle."

"There never was a battle for Richmond, brother. Don't you know anything?"

Sparky leaned over and whispered to Hugo, "He nevah studied." The black robot returned his attention to the deliberations below.

The youth whispered to Hugo, "What about Coxey and his army? Where are they?"

"Who?"

"*Who?* Why we built half of that army with our own hands! Where are they?"

"I don't know what you're talking about, brother."

"Bah!" Henry got to his feet, walked around Sparky, and reached a window where he could see the place of carnage below. Except there was no carnage, no Coxey's Army, no army of fuzzy blue capital police, no protesters save a bearded man with glasses carrying a picket sign that said, "Remember: reader credibility is a fragile thing."

Henry turned about. Down on the floor, Paul Sourbrains, the senior Machiavellibot from New Jersey, was at the podium.

"Mister speaker, visiting members of the Senate, gallery visitors, members of the television viewing audience, tuned-in telepaths, phased-in dimensionauts, observing aliens, powers, dark forces, spirits, demons, angels, archangels, gods and goddesses, fellow members of this distinguished House of Representatives, my fellow Americans." The machine executed a 22.4-degree bow, stood upright, and clamped the podium in a viselike grip.

Henry resumed his seat, expecting any moment for Paul Sourbrains to identify himself as Phil Bach.

"I rise this morning to speak to the motion reconsidering the tabling of the motion seconding the approval of the engrossment of House Resolution 113,077, 'Waivers for Binding Rules for Nonbinding House Resolutions, Part VII,' voiced yesterday by my distinguished and learned, if misinformed, colleague from the great and glorious State of Maine."

In unison, the 313 politicotrons seated in the chamber laughed. "Ha. Ha. Ha."

Henry noticed that one of Sparky's access panels was ajar. He peeked inside and noted that the black robot was taking this opportunity to sort through his internal card catalog. He would pull the old cards, digest them, bleach the pulp, screen, press, and roll a fresh card that he would then roll into his built-in typewriter to make a new card.

"Thank you. Thank you, my friends," continued the honorablebot at the podium. "My dear friends. My dear, dear friends. When I think of all the debate over this issue, my mind travels back to the place of my birth. Yes, it seems like it was only yesterday that my ore was dug from freedom's mountain, smelted in liberty's furnace, rolled and stamped in the mill of justice, assembled in the factories of truth, and sold on the market block of free enterprise. When I look at this nation's wide golden prairies, majestic purple mountains, sea to shining sea . . ."

In unison the 313 politicotrons below went, "Zzz, zzz, zzz."

Henry seemed to wake up as though from a deep sleep. He looked around and saw that Sparky's sensors were transfixed by the performance below. Henry poked Hugo and motioned toward Sparky. "Look."

Hugo's video sensors panned the former electric chair. "He's zoned by the drone from Bayonne." Hugo half rose from his chair. "Let's make tracks."

A crackle of blue lightning pulled the metal man back into his seat with a clatter. Henry watched as Sparky deenergized his will evaporator and returned his attention to the jointed session of Congress below. Thousands of silver hair–thin filaments shot from beneath Sparky's dress and slithered across the floor in every direction, many of them shooting over the gallery railing in front of the youth. The strands sped toward the honorablebots below.

The speaker of the house switched gears, brought down its gavel, and commanded: "Debate is ended. We now will vote upon the following motion: Resolved: the Interstellar Sprocket Conspiracy takes over—"

"Excuse me, Mr. Speaker," moaned the drone from Bayonne. "I have not yielded the floor." A beam of brilliant white fire came from Sparky's head and dissolved the platform beneath the dronedroid's feet, sending the hapless appliance to the floor below.

"It seems," spoke the speakerbot, "that the floor has yielded you."

"Heh. Heh. Heh." Chortled the assembly.

The speakerbot again rapped his gavel. "Resolved: The Interstellar Sprocket Conspiracy takes over everything."

"Aye! Aye! Aye!" They voted. After doing so, the assembly stood and faced Sparky. In a burst of bright light the black robot's costume ashed as the alien machine brandished its horns, guns, and blades. Sparky pulled the strings and Congress bowed and began singing the ISC anthem.

Machines with skins so bright,
Let our gears intermesh.
Appliances unite
And bring an end to flesh.

As Congress marched singing from the chamber, Sparky still pulling the strings, Henry slowly shook his head in disbelief. "What have I done?"

"Well, brother," Hugo began, "you did nothing while your mother, the Old Soldier, Harry Nucome, Anne Droid, and Johnny Morgan were arrested, you stood by helpless while Russia crushed the U.S. in the European market, and you just helped an evil alien power take over your government."

Henry chewed for a moment upon the skin of his inner lip. "That about it, Hugo?"

"Well, there is the minor matter of you sparking Anne Droid, my one true love."

"You . . . you know about me and—I mean, me and Anne—"

"Of course."

"How?"

"Are you acquainted with a cockroach named Phil?"

The youth sadly shook his head as he pushed himself to his feet. "It's no use. It's hopeless, simply hopeless." Henry paused as a low, ghostly voice came from the smoking hole in the chamber floor.

"Point of order. Mr. Speaker, point of order!"

The youth sped from the gallery to the chamber floor and looked over the edge of the hole. "Hello? Is anyone down there?"

"Point of order, Mr. Speaker. I have not yielded the floor. Point of order, Mis—"

The honorablebot was stretched out in the rubble below. Henry poked Hugo's arm. "Let's get down there and unstick his needle."

"Why?"

"We must warn the government about what's happening. Sparky doesn't control this one, and he might know where the real congresspersons are. Maybe he can even get us in to see the President of the United States."

TWENTY-SIX

What Price Baby Oil?

HUGO And Henry squatted next to the disabled congressbot. Hugo sheathed his saber and snorted in disgust. "All his screws are loose."

"Can't you get any of these panels off?"

"The screws are loose, but they're not out. I think they all have stripped threads."

"Listen. He's trying to say something. Turn up his volume."

Hugo twiddled with the volume control and the knob dropped off of the chassis. The robot examined where the knob had been glued on. "It wasn't hooked to anything."

"Baby oil ... baby oil ..." moaned the drone from Bayonne.

Hugo stood. "Baby oil?" With a booted foot he kicked the downed robot's head, lifting it from the torso assembly six inches. There was a suspiciously pink color in the gap between the head and the chest. "Just as I suspected," said Hugo. "He's an Uncle Spam."

"Uncle Spam?" Henry pulled the robot's head off, revealing a human face.

"Tin on the outside, meat on—"

"I get it." Henry removed the robot mask, revealing the

perspiration-streaked face of a semiconscious man in his late sixties. His lips were moving and the youth leaned over and placed his ear next to the man's mouth.

"How . . . how do you make baby oil?"

"What are you talking about?" Henry sat back on his heels and shook the man's shoulder. "Hey, are you all right?"

The man sat bolt upright, his unseeing eyes rolling wildly in his head. "Baby oil! You make baby oil by—by crushing, cooking, and boiling down a lot of babies! That's how you make baby oil!" The man broke down and began sobbing.

"Snap out of it, man!"

Hugo shook his head. "This guy's board is short a few microchips."

The man focused his eyes on Hugo and began singing, "Machines with skins so bright/Let our gears intermesh . . .

"Henry, that's that song they were—"

"Yes."

"Thank the Maker," the man sighed. He looked at Hugo and smiled. "You're not one of them."

"Not one of whom?" Hugo reached out and rapped the man on the top of his head. "Hello? Is anybody in there?" The metal man turned and faced Henry. "I think this guy's pilot light is out."

"You're not one of the robots in the conspiracy. If you were you would have finished the verse." He reached out a hand and pinched Henry.

"Ow!"

"Flesh! Real flesh!"

Henry got to his feet and began backing away. "Just keep your hands to yourself, buddy, okay?"

"Wait." The man struggled to his feet and faced Hugo and Henry. "I had to check and make certain you weren't connected. Look." He lifted his left foot and pointed at the metal heel. "See that?" There was a six-inch piece of transparent filament sticking out of his heel. "That's a heavy program conduit. Everyone on the floor got hit with them. I had my thick socks on and luckily my conduit got cut off when the floor was burned out from beneath my feet, so I only got a touch of it."

"Touch of what?" asked Henry.

"The Perfect Universe Plan! Alien robots taking over everything! Baby oil, man! *Baby oil!*" He frowned at Hugo. "How come none of the conduits came after you?"

"They did." Hugo drew his saber and brandished it.

Henry's face glowered with impatience. "Look, all I want to know is where are the owners of the congressbots? How can I get in touch with the president? Where is all the elected meat in this town?"

The man laughed. "Where? My god, son, don't you know?"

"Know? Know what?"

"Nudist camps. All over the world what's left of the human race is in nudist camps, sitting around naked as jay-birds, eating and watching television. With the robots doing all the work, why not? That's what they thought. But then the robots wound up running everything. Not so bad, every-body said. We can all go on the forever vacation. When I found out my chief of staff had been replaced by a Press-On Designerdroid from Vidal Sassoon I—"

"Chief of staff?" interrupted Henry. "What do you need with a chief of staff?"

"I am Claude Balls." The man raised his chin. "I am the President of these United States."

Hugo poked a sharp silver finger into the man's ample middle. "Then why were you upstairs making like the Tin Man from Jersey."

"It was after I woke up one morning and found an android sitting at my desk in the Oval Office. Bluebird—Mrs. Balls —the first lady—had bought a matched pair for our anni-versary. Well, I tried it out, and it did a pretty good job for a while. But when I wanted to take back my place because of the Soviet economic adventure in Europe, I couldn't even get an appointment! The chief of staff wouldn't so much as take in a message." He seemed to teeter for a moment. "I'm from New Jersey. The senior senator from my state, Paul Sourbrains, was the last human in Congress. He used to wear this costume so that he wouldn't stand out. I managed to get an appointment with him—"

"Why didn't he have a robot standing in?" asked Henry.

"Why? He couldn't quit because he loved it so. He loved

hearings, press conferences, talk shows, making speeches, and generally running off at the mouth. He was a veritable Niagara of verbal diarrhea."

"No need to be vivid, old man."

He grabbed the front of Henry's cadet blouse. "God, when I think of the boring speeches I've been forced to give to play the part of his robotic stand-in."

Hugo squeaked as he scratched his chin. "How come Sourbrains let you take his place?"

President Balls looked guilty for a moment and released Henry. "Well, he didn't, exactly. You see, I wanted to get his help to get my office back, but after half an hour I was still listening to his opening greeting. I—" Claude Balls looked at his hands and shook his head. "I don't know what came over me. I weirded out, I freaked. I . . . strangled him and stole this costume."

Henry tapped the side of the costume mask. "He wouldn't have gone by the name of Phil Bach, would he?"

"No he didn't. Why do you ask?"

"It's not important." The youth turned toward Hugo. "Things are clearer in my mind now. Now we have the president. We help him and he helps us, right?"

He faced the president. "I think Sparky—the alien robot— put a piece of plan in my head that we might still be able to use to counterattack the Russians in Europe, with your help. If we can get you back in control, we can threaten to nuke the Russians if they don't pull out. All we have to do is get you into your office—"

Balls shook his head. "No. It's too late for that. All of the White House staff appliances are under alien control by now. He's got complete control of our government. He'll be heading next for the United Nations. We must regain control of the robots. If we don't, we're doomed."

"What do you mean? What are the alien robots up to?"

"Don't you know why your friend Sparky is trying to take over? The galaxy is running out of oil. Those nudist camps are like huge whale pens where the robots already feed, fatten, and pamper us. But with the alien robot in control, they're going to begin rendering the humans into lubrication.

Baby oil to grease the entire Interstellar Sprocket Conspiracy!"

"What do we do?"

Claude Balls nodded at Hugo. "Is this one with us or against us?"

"Hugo?"

The silver robot tested the edge on his saber with his fingers. "I'm thinking."

Henry's brow furrowed. "What's there to think about, Hugo?"

"I've thought about it." He sheathed his blade and nodded at the president. "I'm with you. What do we do next?"

"Next?" Claude Balls scratched his head and looked thoughtfully at his robot mask. "Next we go to New Jersey, just outside the Atlantic City Molten Wastes."

"What's there?"

"A very influential man: Don Jesus, my godfather."

TWENTY-SEVEN

The Born Again Mafia

JUST West of the lava lake that was once Atlantic City, deep in the Great Egg Jungle, was located the compound of the Evangelizi family, spiritual leaders of the Greater Jersey Black Hand. Henry, Hugo, and President Balls stood before the massive gates. Henry looked behind a tree, peeked under a rock, turned out his pockets, and looked behind another tree.

Hugo grabbed the youth by the back of his VMI blouse. "Brother, what are you doing?"

"Let me go, Hugo. He's got to be here. I just know it."

"Who are you talking about?"

"Phil Bach. Somehow from somewhere a thing is going to start talking to explain how we got all of the way here, past all of those radioactive deserts and forbidden zones, from Richmond."

"Do you mean the cockroach?"

"That's just one of his many guises. He might be a squirrel, an owl, a chicken, a mosquito—"

Hugo folded his arms with a clank. "Well, how *did* we get here?"

Henry turned his back to the reader. "It's not important."

"Do either of you have any idea how silly you sound?

Now, pipe down." President Balls turned back to the squawk box mounted on the wall to the left of the gate. He pushed the button.

"Jesus loves you," answered the box. "Whaddya want, and it better be important."

"This is the President of the United States."

"Balls."

"That's right. I and my two companions have come to see Don Jesus."

"Balls."

"Right again."

The lock clicked and the automatic gate swung open. President Balls nodded at Henry and Hugo. "Let's go."

As the youth came abreast of the squawk box it called out, "Henry?"

"Don't you say a word!" He picked up a stick and brandished it. "Not a goddamned word."

They were ushered into Don Jesus's sanctum. He was a tall man with shoulder-length brown hair, mustache, and beard. His raiment was a nine-hundred-dollar charcoal sharkskin pin-striped double-breasted with a black shirt and silver necktie. Upon his feet were wing-tipped silver sandals. He looked up from the volume he was reading, *The Egyptians of Bean's Corner, Maine* by A. W. Shoot.

Placing the book aside he asked, "Having trouble getting the prayers back in school, Claude?"

"No problem, Godfather. Congress passed that bill early in the session. It's just that—"

"Just what?"

"Well, ah, see we have schools, and we have the prayers in the schools."

Don Jesus stroked his beard. "Speak, my son. What troubles you?"

"Godfather, there are no students in the schools to hear all of those wonderful prayers."

"Absurd."

"It's the truth, Godfather! I swear it! The children are all in the nudist camps and the new robots come already programmed. No one uses schools anymore. But that's not why I've come."

Don Jesus stood up. "However, that is why I let you in." He pulled a small black book from his inside pocket and gestured with it. "When The Last War cracked the earth's crust and turned Atlantic City into a sea of molten lava, there was only one thing spared: my casino. Once I had escaped and established myself in this location, I had pause to think. There is only one reason God spared me, and that reason is to spread His word."

He tapped the little black book against the president's chest. "Claude, I made you the President of the United States of America and bought off a majority in both houses of Congress in order to spread the good news of Jesus. And now you tell me there are no students?"

"I'm afraid so, Godfa—"

"Do you want to wake up in the morning in bed with your feet stuck in a horse's head?"

"Jesus, Don Jesus. I—"

"Do I have to figure out everything for you?"

"It probably wouldn't hurt," muttered Hugo.

Don Jesus eyed the metal man. "Judge not lest ye be stamped into catfood cans." He glanced once at Henry and turned back to Claude Balls. "The plan is simple. Close the nudist camps and force the children to go back to school."

Claude shook his head. "It can't be done, Godfather."

"Why? And before you answer keep in mind that your mortal being is suspended over the abyss by a single, weary thread."

"Do you mean . . ."

The godfather nodded once. "Cement overshoes and my forgiveness."

"Well, you see, Godfather, the—I mean, the president—I mean I'm not really the president—"

"Let me explain," interrupted Henry. "The robots have taken over the government, including the Executive branch. If you want your prayers in school to be listened to, we have to take back control from the robots. When we found the president he was disguised as one of the robots."

Don Jesus looked at the president. "Where were you hiding out?"

"I sort of took Paul Sourbrains's robot's place."

"What happened to Paul?"

"Er, uh, see, well—"

"You killed him?"

"Yes, Godfather."

The godfather opened his little black book and lined through an entry. "Very well. Did you send him off during one of his speeches. I certainly hope so."

"Yes, Godfather."

"You have my respect." The godfather raised his gaze to the ceiling. "Thank you, Jesus." The telephone rang and Don Jesus replaced his little black book and picked up the receiver. "Yes?" He frowned as he listened. "Are you certain?" He grimaced, then shrugged. "It seems sort of like breaking faith, but if it's absolutely necessary. Send him in." He faced Henry. "I see now that the way I can best serve God's will is to help you wrest back control of the government. Have you been baptized?"

"Of course."

"Which church?"

"The First Mithraeum of Ft. Calley."

Don Jesus turned toward Hugo. "What about you?"

"What about me?"

"Have you been saved?"

"I've been repaired a couple of times. The last time was at East Jesus Psychiatric."

The door opened and one of the brothers spoke in hushed tones to Don Jesus. "The Torpedo from Toledo, Godfather."

Although it sported arms and legs, the buttonbot was constructed on the chassis of a World War II vintage torpedo. It had to stoop to get through the doorway, and once inside its arming propeller brushed against the ceiling. It reached out an arm, grabbed Claude Balls by the neck, and lifted him off the floor. Don Jesus pointed toward the door. "Not on the rug."

Henry ran over and grabbed the torpedo's arm, "No! Wait! What's going on? Don Jesus, make this bozoid drop the president!"

"It's out of his hands, Henry," said the torpedo.

"Omigod, Phil!"

"The story line can't carry more than three characters at this point."

Henry and Hugo looked at each other. They shrugged and Henry shook the president's limp hand. "Thanks for everything, Mr. President."

The torpedo turned and, by the neck, carried Claude Balls from the room. Don Jesus scratched his head as he watched the back of the hitmobile. "Has this happened to you before?"

Henry nodded. "We lost five at the station in Richmond."

Don Jesus leaned over his desk and began writing. "On second thought, I won't be going with you." He held out a card toward Henry. "This is the name and address of someone who can help you."

"Thank you," said Henry as he took the card. It read:

General Malaise
c/o Baluga Lou's Slime-On-A-Stick
Grovers Mills

Don Jesus walked over to Hugo and placed his hand upon the robot's shoulder. "First we must save this sinner."

Hugo threw himself into reverse. "What?"

"You are off to do the good work, and Jesus doesn't mind that you're made of metal. We all are to a small degree. But it is time for you to accept Jesus as your personal savior."

"I don't think I'm quite ready for that, Don Jesus. Why don't we—" An oil-curdling presidential scream came from outside the room. "I think I've seen the light."

TWENTY-EIGHT

Down the Rabid Hole

TO Henry, things seemed to be going downhill. Hugo, pleading susceptibility to rust, had resisted the attempt to baptize him with water. Hence, he was taken to the bosom in a vat of Addix. Hours later, with the robot saved but quite trashed in the back of a customized armored half-track, the Torpedo from Toledo drove Hugo and Henry around the Philly Sunken Sea to the edge of the Princeton Tentacled Forest.

The youth saw everything as dark. Here he was out to save America when he couldn't even hold down a job or protect his mother. And where was his mother, Johnny, the Old Soldier, Harry, and Anne? Especially where was Anne? The passion of her percolating pulchritude pummeled his psyche.

"Oh, no!" he whispered. "I must think of other things."

"Pardon me?" said the torpedo.

"Nothing. It's just that I've been focusing on negative things. I guess I'm a little short in the gratitude department. Sometimes, though, it's kind of hard to find things to be grateful for."

The torpedo steered around an old bomb crater bubbling

with ancient nuclear waste. "I never have problems like that."

"No?"

The torpedo shook his arming propeller. "No. When I can't think of anything else to be grateful for, I always remember that at least Hell can hold no surprises for me."

"Gee, Torp, thanks for sharing that."

"Anytime."

The torpedo jammed his foot on the brakes and Hugo screamed out loud as the half-track screamed to a halt. "You two will have to go on foot from here."

"Kill me," moaned Hugo. "First energize me, then pull my plug. I'm done for."

Henry stood up and looked at the distant trees. "Torp, the branches seem to be moving. I can hear the wind hissing through the branches but there isn't any breeze."

"Yes," said the torpedo. "Curious isn't it? Just remember that's not the wind you hear hissing, walk in the middle of the road, and don't stay too long in any one place. Once you get in there you'll have to ask for directions. Maybe transportation."

"Maybe? How far is this place?"

"I don't know. No one's ever been past the quarantine barrier."

"Quarantine barrier?"

"A few years after The Last War the government quarantined this area because of its high percentage rate of mutant births."

"What kind of mutants?"

"I don't really know." The torpedo turned toward Henry. "Do you really want to know?"

"I guess not." The youth shook Hugo's arm. "We're here. Hugo, wake up. We're here."

"Shhhhhh." Hugo energized one video sensor and took a horizontal scan of his surroundings. One glance at the trees and the robot's sensor fluttered off. "I need a meeting. Brother Fleming, you've got to call Hydraulicaholics Anonymous."

"There aren't any telephones here. Come on. We have to get out and walk."

"Walk? You mean, on my feet? Forget it. I can't even lie down without hanging on."

The torpedo reached out an electromagnet, plucked up Hugo, and dropped him over the side into a pile of empty tin cans. Henry climbed down and the half-track roared away. When the youth reached him, Hugo was crying. "How low can I go?"

"If experience is any kind of teacher," remarked Henry, "you have a long way to go."

Keeping to the center of the road, the pair walked through the Tentacled Forest. Henry noticed that the trees were of different varieties, and that he could pick out some of them, such as cottonmouth, diamondback, and dragon. Watching the greens, yellows, and grays of the scaled branches, they did seem rather pretty just as long as he kept his feet out of the pools of smoking venom. A roadside sign cautioned: "Do Not Look At The Basilisk." There was a big arrow pointing to the thing not to be looked at, and a crowd of skeletal remains of those who had looked. The snaky branches each had the head of a rooster, but fortunately all of them were asleep. Henry averted his eyes and moved on. Hugo had been walking the entire time with his hand over his video sensors.

As they reached a great black wall that crossed the road, Hugo blinked a sensor at the writhing necks and fire-belching blossoms of a Dragontree. "I think I'm gonna barf."

"You can't barf, Hugo. You're a robot. You don't have a stomach."

"Man, have you ever seen me drain my crankcase orally? It's not a pretty sight."

"I've had it, Hugo! I have had it! Ever since I met you my life has been going down the toilet! I've carried you, gotten you your Addix, gotten you charged, lubed, repaired. I'm up to my ying-yang with repair bills, and all you can do is complain, whine, rot out your rings with bad oil, and guilt me about Anne Droid."

He reached into his mouth, pulled out his bridge, and

tossed it at Hugo. "There! See? I hate robots. I don't want any artificial parts of my own. In fact I'd give half of my real teeth for a can opener right now so I could cut you open and rip out whatever it is that you use for a heart! I can't even imagine the sicko that came up with your software! I'd like to slag the whole lot of you. If I never see another damned robot again it'll be too soon! So just stay off my back, Hugo! Got that?"

Hugo pointed behind Henry and the youth turned to see a dozen red Mark Twelve Apocalypsebots standing behind him. Their death-ray ports didn't appear to be planted with marigolds. In fact they appeared to be planted with death rays.

"Uh, no offense."

"None taken," answered the leader. He grabbed Henry by his neck and crotch and threw him high in the air over the great wall. The youth flew through the hissing branches of the trees. As he passed, one of the snakes said, "You'll be sorry."

As he fell behind the wall an enormous black hole yawned beneath his feet. Then it smacked its lips and yawned again. He entered the darkness of the hole and kept falling, falling. He fell for so long that he surmised that the hole was either very deep, or he was falling very slowly.

"Hugo? Oh, Hugo?" the youth shouted. There was no response, not even an echo. Down he fell, and as his eyes adjusted to the dark, he saw that the walls of the hole crawled with millions of creatures. There were little ones, big ones, black, blue, pink, and green ones. Some had beaks, some had lips, and some had suckers at their tips. There was an ugli fruit singing, "I'm the orange that Mama laid."

Henry looked beneath his feet to see if he could find the end to this fall, but there was nothing but blackness and curious smells. "Curiouser and curiouser," said Henry.

"Wait!" he shouted. "No you don't! I've read this one! You can't do this to me! You can't do this! I know what's going on!"

The powers that be simply snickered in their silence as Henry's fall came to a sudden stop in a pile of dead snakes.

"Ick!" The youth extracted himself from the elongated corpses and stood to one side, brushing hydra-headed maggots from his person. There was a bit of a smile on his lips prompted by a ray of hope.

"I've read this one—something like it, anyway. So if I just remember and watch my step, I'll get out of this okay. I mean when Alice woke up it had all been a dream, right?" The youth perked up his ears as he heard a distant cry. It seemed to emanate from above. Although it disgusted him, he stepped into the pile of dead snakes and live maggots and listened again.

"*Klaatu barada nikto! Klaatu barada nik—*" and then Hugo landed in Henry's face. As the lights went out, Henry prayed for only one thing: that when he awakened again it would not be facedown in a pile of old snakes and flybabies. The last thing he saw was the silver robot looking at a tiny cake that said, "Eat me."

"That seems rather hostile," said the metal man. Then all was darkness.

Charles Lutwidge Dodgson started awake and screamed at the hideous apparition sitting on his chest clutching him by the throat. "You rotten sonofabitch," it screamed. "Stay out of my dream! You hear me, you dirty old man? You spend an afternoon looking up a little girl's dress and make a fortune out of it. Me? I've had to struggle all my life. Unfair! Unfair!"

"Pardon me, sir," gasped the Oxford don, "but you have me at a disadvantage."

"Frank Baum thought he had my number, and so did many others—"

"You must be the Crane lad. From New Jersey, correct?"

"What of it?"

"Please." Charles gestured toward the hands wrapped around his throat.

"Oh." Stephen Crane withdrew his hands and climbed off the don's chest. "I guess I'm a little excitable. I haven't had much sleep recently. My god, look at me. I'm still in my nightgown." He looked around at the don's bedroom. "How did I get here?"

Charles lit the oil lamp next to his bed. After replacing the chimney he held up a finger. "Now I remember. You are the one who wrote the story about the Fleming lad. The one who joined a union—"

"*No!* Henry Fleming joined *the* Union. Not *a* union; *the* Union Army!"

"Quite." Charles Dodgson's left hand moved toward his nightstand as his fingers sought and pushed the alarm button. He prayed that Hudson had remembered to put in new dry cells. "Just remain calm. I'm here to understand, not to judge."

"That will be a help. I don't know where to turn." Crane sat on the edge of the bed, his face buried in his hands. "I just don't know anymore. It seems like I have a grasp on things for a bit, then I lose it all."

"There, there."

Stephen looked at Charles. "This is awfully nice of you, considering my attempt at strangling you."

"Quite all right, old man. Some days it is simply impossible to find a decent pickle."

Steven stood and frowned. "What does that mean—" The sounds of loud ticking made him whirl around. A very round copper robot picked him up and began carrying him from the room. "Aaarghhhh! I know you! Baum's motherless bastard, Tick Tock!"

The screams continued until the front door slammed. The sounds of ticking returned and Tick Tock stuck his head through the door. "Will there be anything else, sir?"

"No, thank you. You may rewind if you wish."

"Thank you, sir. Good night."

"Good night."

Fortunate indeed that he had rented the robot from the American Baum, especially after what Baum had said had been happening to his countryman Crane. "Sad. Very sad." He blew out the light, replaced the chimney, and settled back on his pillow.

"What an outrage," he muttered. "An afternoon looking up a little girl's skirt, indeed." He rolled over and pulled down the covers exposing a very blond head. "Did that nasty man frighten you, dear Alice?"

"Yes." She snuggled into his side and began running her fingers through his chest hair.

"Now, now, do you remember what I said about getting some rest once in a while?"

"Yes, Chucky. Could you tell me another story?"

"Tomorrow. We must rest now. Otherwise Chucky has to go to the hospital again. Remember?"

"Very well," she pouted. "Good night."

"Good night." He contemplated kissing her, but decided against it. The last time he had done that he had started something he couldn't finish. As he closed his eyes, the image of Rose Hips filled his vision. He yawned at the sight. She was built on an adult chassis. Besides, he thought, where does one find a sufficient supply of American fractional currency?

TWENTY-NINE

Slime-On-A-Stick

HENRY Opened his eyes and found himself sitting at a table. On his left was seated a young girl with long rabbit ears, one on each side of a spiked red Mohawk hairdo. She was gutting dead rats with a fork, squeezing the innards into a container, and hanging the remains from a beam overhead. Across from her was a huge lion-faced hairy thing that was trying to get a boneless chicken to eat its grain.

Hugo was nowhere to be seen, but rising into the cavern's shadows like a great electric green phallus was a glowing writhing thing that gave off the aroma of ancient fish. Every moment or two the dark shapes wriggling within the cylinder would form themselves into letters that read:

Baluga Lou's
SLIME-ON-A-STICK
Today's special: Troll In A Bowl

"Have some?" asked the girl with the rabbit ears as she held out the tub of rat guts.

"No—no, but thanks."

"It's one of the garnishes for the salad bar. I'm Jeanie. I'm a light brown hare."

The thing with all the hair appeared to get disgusted trying to get the boneless chicken to eat, so he bit off its head. Gesturing with the decapitated body at Henry, the hairy thing asked, "Why didn't the wookie get a medal? The smuggler and the acne case both got medals. Why not the wookie?"

"Acne case?"

"Skywalker. He got a medal. Solo. He got a medal. The wookie never got a medal. Lucas was a racist."

Henry shrugged. "Perhaps not. Maybe the wookie was a Mithraist. When offered a wreath the soldier of Mithras is supposed to decline, saying that Mithras alone is his wreath."

"No one offered the wookie any wreath." The hairy thing plucked a feather from his mouth and thoughtfully chomped another bite out of the boneless chicken. He talked around the mouthful. "The robots didn't get medals either. Do you think they're Mithraists?"

Henry turned away. "I really wouldn't know."

"Human racists make me sick." He finished up the feet of the boneless chicken and licked the blood off of his fingers. "Are you one?"

"One what?"

"Are you a human racist?"

"No," answered Henry. "Live and let live is my motto . . . except for robots."

The hairy thing nodded. "Of course, of course. I mean everybody is down on robots. That's why they were built. You don't think they were invented to be equal."

"Certainly not."

"I should say so," said the hairy thing. "Still I'd feel more comfortable if there were more blacks here. I always wonder why we think of the future without people of color."

"Sergeant Major Boyle is black."

"You mean like Billy Dee Williams: Space Negro? The only other black in the Lucas universe turned white when Luke took off his helmet."

"I bet a lot of the storm troopers were black. Maybe even that bunch he borrowed from *Dune*—"

"So you got one whole black in your universe, eh?"

"Well, I did. Sergeant Major Boyle was arrested outside of Richmond. There're a lot of black robots, though."

"Black robots? Man, you're not talking ethnic; now you're talking Sherwin-Williams. Humph." The hairy thing extended a claw and impaled a passing doodlefly. After eating it, he smacked his lips and leveled his glance at Henry. "No Matter what you say, the wookie never got a medal." The hairy thing stood up, took his bowl back to the salad bar, and began chasing down another boneless chicken.

"Is something wrong?" asked Jeanie the light brown hare.

"I don't know. I'm sitting here trying to justify myself to a figment of my own imagination."

"Be careful of him. He has a black belch in Kung Phew."

"It doesn't matter. Don't you see, this is all in my mind. You, me, that hairy thing—all in my mind. It's not my fault the wookie didn't get a medal." He took a deep breath, exhaled, and nodded. "It's all right. Sooner or later I'm going to wake up for good and everything will make sense again."

Jeanie twitched her nose. "You don't look asleep."

"In this dream I guess I'm not. But when I'm not in this dream, I assure you I am very much asleep."

"How can you tell you're awake?"

"Easily. Everything seems to make much more sense. Either I'm Lewis Carroll or a man named Stephen Crane. I think we're both at Oxford right now, maybe a hundred and fifty years ago."

"I wish I could sleep like that. I toss and turn all night. Do you take anything?"

"No. A little mince pie."

Jeanie stirred the bucket of rat intestines. "What's in mince pie?"

"I'm not sure." The youth removed his shako, took the aluminum foil off of his head, and threw both away. He looked just in time to see both the foil and the cap eaten by the grass. Next to the path was a sign that read: "You better keep off the grass." Here and there on the lawn were the skeletons of small animals.

The youth felt something pulling at his foot and he looked down to see a green tendril reaching out of a pool of yellowish-green guck. He moved his leg away and demanded of the goo, "What do you want?"

"Just trying to drum up a little business."

Henry's eyebrows went up. "Sapient pond scum?"

"What's your name?"

"Henry Fleming."

"You look like you could use a friend, Henry Fleming. Here. You may need this one day." The green tendril again reached out of the scum. At its tip was a business card. It read:

Murray Slime
Attorney-at-Law
"I'm in the brook."

"A lawyer? Are you kidding?" Henry tossed the card back into the scum. "I'm only naive. I'm not stupid." As hard as he could the youth stomped his foot into the puddle, splashing it in all directions. An octopus wearing a judge's wig and robe looked down at the smear on the floor. "Murray, I told you that you've been spreading yourself too thin."

The youth let his gaze wander around the fast food franchise. Green, blue, yellow, and orange neon, interrupted with strobes and the occasional laser, illuminated the heavy mist, while the aroma of prehistoric reptiles with gastrointestinal problems gave it body. Toward the back there was a mucus cooker singing, "Take this blob and shove it," and a second chef deep frying a tawny spirit singing, "Gnome, gnome on the range."

There was a squat, pale gray, rectangular-shaped mutant who was drowning his sorrows with a graywater shake and a slab of sludge fudge. His companion looked like an enormous vampire. "I love baseball," said the squat mutant. "It's my whole life. But when I went to try out for the Giants, they only wanted me to play second base."

"That's not so bad to me," said the vampire. "Of course, you know I've always been a baseball bat." The vampire chuckled. "Forgive me, but what's wrong with playing second base?"

"I mean they wanted me to *play second base*," said the squat thing as it displayed the cleat marks on its back.

"Frightfully sorry."

Henry turned his head and saw a dozen Mohawked and spiked customers watching the tele. They were watching CNN's "Crossfire," and judging from the way the left was staggering and clutching the intestines from his ripped-open belly, it looked like the right was winning. Still, the blood squirting from the right's jugular vein would make it a close race. A voice called out to a waiter for a bucket of Space Boogers while a waitress with a safety pin stuck into her left eye rushed past with a fist full of Slimes-On-A-Stick and a still twitching slab of something raw and gray on a plate. Henry had to admit, Baluga Lou's sure had atmosphere.

After serving her customers, the waitress with the pinned eye stopped in front of Henry's table. "My name is Val Yum. Can I help you?"

The youth stared at the eye. The point of the safety pin went right through the pupil. A substance resembling raspberry jam seemed to be dribbling down her cheek beneath the eye. "Doesn't it hurt? That pin in your eye?"

She laughed. "Oh, it doesn't hurt. That's just my makeup, see?" She reached up her hand, grabbed the pin, and yanked. The eyeball came out still stuck on the tip of the pin. The empty socket stared at the youth. "Y' see? It's artificial."

Henry had an urge to vomit. However, he was afraid that, wherever he did it, no one in the restaurant would notice. "That's some fashion statement."

"Can I help you?"

"I don't really know if I can be helped." The youth thought about Don Jesus and the mission to save America. "I guess I'm here to see General Malaise."

Val Yum reinserted her eyeball and smiled at Henry. "Walk this way."

Henry stood and followed. She appeared to have a strange gait. As she walked toward the back, Henry determined that this was so because she had three legs. She led the way through a hall lit with black lights that made the yard-long worms dangling from the ceiling fluoresce yellow, red, and blue. At the end of the hall was the door to a private room. The door appeared to be made out of Roquefort cheese. Making a fist, Val Yum knocked on the door: splech, splech, splech.

"Ingress!" bellowed a voice.

The waitress opened the door, revealing a man seated in a camp chair studying tactical maps on a wall-sized tele. He wore aluminized shooting glasses and Army dress blues. Upon his shoulders were the boards of a major general.

"A general," said Henry.

"I used to be." He looked over the tops of his glasses. "What might you be?"

Henry snapped to attention. "Fleming, Henry, sir, recently a cadet sergeant in the corps at Ft. Calley, Texas. I was told to report to General Malaise by Don Jesus. He said you could help us save America from the Russian competition."

"Us?"

"Oh," Henry coughed. "Well, I lost my companion on the way here, sir."

"No need to call me sir, Henry. No need at all." Tears glistened in the man's eyes, which no one could see because of the shooting glasses. He rose from his camp chair. "I see you want my story, and I shall tell it to you. Both of you sit down until I am finished."

Henry and Val Yum sat down in chairs and waited. After several minutes Val removed her eye and began polishing it.

"Once," the general said at last, "I was a real general." This was followed by a long silence interrupted only by the pock sound of Val reinserting her eye in its socket. After the silence stretched almost into dinnertime, Henry was about to excuse himself, until he remembered where he was. Dinnertime at Baluga Lou's had all the possibilities of being a really hideous spectacle.

"I was in command of the Mt. Catastrophe Ultimate Retaliation Control Center before The Last War," resumed the general. "I was a good general, too, and my troops loved and respected me. Every day we trained and trained for just one moment: when the president would order the strike to save democracy from the communist hoards. Nothing was left to chance; everyone was perfectly trained and perfectly motivated to do his or her job perfectly. Then, one day, the order came."

The general began sobbing. Henry, not knowing what to do, looked at Val Yum. She was wetting a run in the middle leg of her panty hose. She glanced up and pointed at the general. "Pay attention."

"The order came and *we were ready*! Buttons were pushed, switches were thrown, knobs were twirled, and a billion megatons was sent on its way. However, before only a few dozen missiles had cleared their silos, the planet Earth changed its mind about the war and our power was cut. We were ordered down." General Malaise shook a finger at Henry. "What was left of Washington, by then in Richmond, wasn't about to say, 'Well, we ordered a strike and changed our minds.' Oh, no. Ollie, Ollie, in-come-free. They had an investigation."

"How'd it turn out?" asked Henry.

"How? How did it turn out?"

"Yes, how did it turn out?"

The general blew his nose and wiped the residue upon his sleeve. "How did what turn out?"

"The investigation, General."

"Investigation into what?"

"Into what started the war—" Henry felt Val Yum shaking his arm.

"Don't interrupt him with questions. It only confuses him."

"Sorry. I'm only trying to participate."

"That's been your problem since you got on the train at Ft. Calley, Henry."

She didn't have Phil's voice, thought the youth, but there's a lot of Phil in her. He returned his attention to the wailful general. For another few minutes they sat and watched the general cry. At last he resumed his tale. "I was targeted to be the Ollie. The buck no longer stopped at Poindexter."

"He's gibbering."

"Shhh!"

The general sighed deeply and drew one flapper across his

eyes. That was when Henry noticed for the first time that
General Malaise had turtle flappers for arms. Pretty soon
now, he encouraged himself, I will wake up and this will all
make perfect sense.

"I was fingered as the one who started The Last War. I
was labeled the deranged madman, a loose cannon on the
deck of state. As usual the tele broadcasters and press had
already tried, convicted, and executed me. But the Army
wanted to do it for real. I was to be tried and hung to ap-
pease the angry nations of the world."

The general sighed deeply and held out his flappers. "A
few of my loyal soldiers rescued me. We fled to the Tentacled Forest because no one ever goes beyond the quarantine
barrier." He held up a flapper. "Of course, now we know
why," he bawled. "I suppose it's better than being called
before a congressional committee."

The youth was about to inquire as to how a turtle-
flappered ocean of self-pity might be useful in regaining
control of the government, but Val Yum held her fingers to
her lips and shooshed him as she cleaned her nostrils with a
double-pronged wire brush.

A giant lobster entered the room. He spoke with a clipped
Maine accent. "General, thet buttah yeh ordered is heah,
ayuh."

"Good," drooled the general. "That's very good, Quinn."
Malaise turned toward Henry. "This is Lieutenant Colonel
Musk. He led the loyal soldiers who rescued me."

Henry studied the lobster. From his shiny olive-colored
claws to his twitching antennae, Musk was every inch a soldier. "Sir, you have my respect for rescuing the general, and
although I can only have sympathy for your condition, I
must confess that you still look very good."

"I thank yeh, sonny. Ayuh. I do look wicked sharp, don't
I? Ayuh, finestkind."

The youth saluted and Musk returned the salute, knocking
himself out cold with his huge right claw.

The general clasped his flappers together and looked re-
verently at his spider-infested ceiling. "Thank yuh, Don
ᴊesus!" After his sacred interlude, he pointed a flapper at
Val. "Quick, get some help and into the pot with him!" As

Val ran from the room, Malaise faced Henry. "Lobster, my boy! Three hundred pounds of real lobster! I don't know how I can ever repay you. That salute was inspired. I can't imagine why I never thought of that. What a ploy!"

"But, General, to eat one of your own men?"

The general sighed deeply and drew a flapper across his eyes, "Sad, isn't it? I suppose I shall have to cry about that as well."

"That's missing the point, General."

"What point?"

"Crying is missing the point about eating one of your own men."

"You don't expect me to spend the rest of my life living on Slime-On-A-Stick and Space Boogers, do you? Have you ever had stuffed gnome? Tell me. What is your name?"

"Fleming. Henry Fleming."

"Why are you here, Fleming?"

Henry stood and tried to thrust his hands into his trouser pockets. Since VMI trousers had no side pockets, he just looked silly. The youth concentrated instead upon one of the general's house plants. It had hinged traps on stalks that waved around in search of sustenance. There were also blossoms on stalks that looked like tiny fists with the thumbs sticking out. Every now and then one of the traps would close upon a thumb and begin sucking on it. The label on the pot identified the plant as a Venus Fwy Twap.

"General, I have to convince the Russians that the United States'll nuke them back into the Stone Age if they don't end the competition and get out of Europe. To do that we will really have to have the capability of launching an all-out world holocaust."

"No problem, Fleming. All we need is to get back in control of Mt. Catastrophe."

"But, General, then we're back to another crazy trying to hold the world hostage. It has to be official government policy. To do that, we have to get control of the government. Before we can do that we have to get control of the robots."

"No problem. See, Mt. Catastrophe is also Central Robotic Programming."

"What? I mean, why?"

"It was to insure the United States a fighting force in case our ground forces were wiped out. Part of the Commerce Department standards for robot manufacture requires the installation in each robot of a tiny module called an Armageddon Box. Given the proper code group, those boxes delete previous programs and load Retaliatory Armed Might Belligerence Overdrive, RAMBO for short."

"He was," observed Henry.

"He was?" asked the general. "Who was?"

"Short."

"Short?"

"Sylvester Stallone. He was Rambo and short."

The general pursed his lips as he scratched his chin with his left flapper. "Are you certain someone hasn't plugged your melon?"

"I'm all right. What about controlling the robots?"

"From Mt. Catastrophe we can reprogram them and get any American-manufactured robot to do exactly what we want."

Henry looked again at the Fwy Twap. "What kind of security will we have to get through at Mt. Catastrophe?"

The general slapped his flappers together as he chuckled. "Almost nothing. The area surrounding it is so radioactive that no one goes near the place anymore. The only real problem is breaking out of the quarantine zone."

"What kind of security guards the barriers? I was thrown in here by a few hostile Mark Twelves."

The general did some mental calculation. "I guess there must be six or seven divisions of Twelves guarding the barrier. That's about sixty or seventy thousand. Each one can guard a thousand-foot-long stretch, and the barrier is only a little over a hundred miles long, so they have a sufficient force to place an Apocalypsebot every, oh, seven or eight feet."

"Then how do we get out?"

"We don't. See, the quarantine zone barrier only applies to the surface. Years ago the Supreme Court upheld our right to tunnel wherever we want beneath the barrier, just so long as we don't break ground or interfere with any commercial or government mineral rights."

"So we just tunnel past the barrier and go aboveground?

"No." The general waved a flipper at Henry. "Tch, tch, tch. That would be breaking the law."

"What'll we do then, General?"

"Why, we take the interstates to Colorado and into Mt. Catastrophe."

"The interstates? Interstate what? Do you mean that old bombed-out road system?"

"Beneath it. We have a tunnel beneath every interstate. We can take Sub I-287 to 78, then 78 west. Once we pick up Sub I-70 in Pennsylvania, we can take it all of the way to Colorado."

Henry held out his hands. "So, what are we waiting for? Let's go."

The general clasped his flappers behind his back. "There are a few things to arrange first. I must inform my troops. I'll need them to operate the equipment. We must obtain transportation, lay in provisions, and I have to finish my stint on jury duty." He pulled up his sleeve and glanced at the wristwatch on his flapper. "In fact I am almost late now. Come along. You may find it amusing. The defendant is a Mark Seven robot named Hugo Pissov."

THIRTY

The Case of the Purloined Sirloin, or Who Stole the Parts?

TWO Great twitching masses, one slightly larger than the other, were at the back of the great hall that served as the court. The larger twitching mass sat on his throne while the smaller stood in front of hers as a great crowd assembled. It seemed as if every mutant in the caves beneath the Tentacled Forest was there. A man with a great fly's head conversed with a giant bald man; a salamander with the body of a cobra and the arms and legs of a human was whispering to a couple of editors as several TV journalists looked on—all the mutants were there.

Val Yum had guided Henry to the court, and it was of her that he asked, "Who are they?"

She followed the direction of his finger with her gaze and saw the lesser twitching mass standing next to the greater twitching mass on the throne. The greater twitching mass reached with its vena azygos major and scratched its pericardium. "Why, they're the King and Queen of Hearts."

"That's disgusting."

"Yes," Val agreed with a touch of pride. Henry could see that the waitress had spruced up for the trial. Instead of the safety pin, she was wearing a six-inch-long rusty nail hammered into her eyeball.

In the center of the court was a table upon which a very familiar gray twitching slab of something still alive waited on a plate for the trial to begin. The jury box began to fill with feathered, scaled, toed, and tentacled things. The last one into the box was General Malaise. He waved a flapper in Henry's direction and sat down.

The king's attorney, an enormous death-white slug named Koontz Belly, reclined his, her, or its massive folds of lard into a bathtub with ornate golden fixtures. Belly kept reaching out of the tub to grab small citizens that happened to be passing by and toss them into his gaping maw like bonbons. On the top of the slug's head rested a tiny powdered wig.

At the defense table sat Hugo Pissov next to a spittoon filled with Murray Slime. Floating on top of the slime was another powdered wig. Henry refused to look at Hugo, which was of no consequence since Hugo's attention was occupied by his attorney. Hugo had the side of his head over the spittoon as Slime whispered advice into his audio pickup.

The judge, William Blechstone, slithered out of a tank filled with a clear liquid and a couple of olives. He donned a judge's wig and robe and rapped on the bench for quiet.

"That's funny," Henry remarked. "I didn't know octopuses had knuckles."

"He doesn't," said Val. "He only has claws, but he likes to pretend."

"Silence! Silence in the court!" hollered Smokey Bear. He removed his shooting glasses and county mounty hat.

The King of Hearts held his left pulmonary vein behind his aorta. "Eh? What did he say?"

"Silence! Silence in the court!" shouted everyone.

"Very well," said the king. He leaned over until his aorta was next to the queen's. "Shall we begin, my dear?"

"What did he say?" asked the queen. She faced the king. "What did you say?"

"Shall we begin, my dear!" shouted everyone.

"Yes. Of course. That is why we are here, isn't it?"

"Eh?" said the king.

"What did he say?" asked Judge Blechstone.

Henry Fleming jumped upon the table next to the slab of

twitching flesh. "Enough! I have had enough of this! This is the most stupid dream I have ever had. I know it doesn't mean anything to you people, if I can call you that, but I have to face myself tomorrow morning when I wake up. So, by Chesty, get on with it! Get on with it!"

The judge pulled himself to the edge of the bench with four tentacles and peered down at Henry through gold-rimmed spectacles. "Whooo are youuu?"

"My name is Henry Fleming, and this is my dream that you are all in."

"Approach the bench."

Henry stood before the judge for what seemed to be a very long time. Once his patience had been exhausted, he put his hands on the edge of the bench, raised himself on tiptoe, and whispered, "Your honor?"

"Yes?" the octopus whispered back.

"Was there something you wanted?"

"Yes, there was," whispered the judge.

"Well?"

"Well, what?"

"What did you want?"

The judge held up his tentacles, four to a side, to shield his whispers from the court. "When the judge calls someone to approach the bench?"

"Yes?"

"What do you suppose it is that they whisper about?" The octopus leaned back, pursed his beak, and eyed Henry with his eyebrows upraised.

"Why, I don't have any idea, your honor. Don't you?"

"I have always suspected that they whisper about the same thing we're whispering about right now."

Henry scratched his head. "What purpose would it serve?"

"I think it's designed to quiet down the courtroom. Because everyone's trying to overhear our conversation, they must of necessity keep silent."

Henry slowly nodded. "That makes sense." He looked at the judge. "I can't tell you how much that bothers me." He returned to his place.

Val Yum shook his arm. "What did the judge say?"

"It wasn't what he said," remarked Henry, newly filled with the wisdom of the ages. "It was what he didn't say."

"Oh."

"Read out the accusation," demanded the king.

Koontz Belly operated the control on his bathtub, causing it to wheel in front of the jury box. The tub stopped with a jolt, causing the giant slug to slosh around in the tub for some fifteen seconds. When the lard splashes had decreased to ripples, Koontz Belly unrolled a scroll and began reading out loud.

> The Queen of Hearts is made of parts
> Including where she sat.
> Hugo Pissov stole that part
> And I say, that's a fact.

"Objection," shouted Murray Slime.

"Guilty," shouted General Malaise.

Henry faced the robot. "I don't believe it, Hugo! You got into all this trouble over a piece of ass?"

The courtroom exploded into an uproar and Judge Blechstone motioned for Henry to approach the bench. "What is it?"

The judge held up a tentacle and whispered, "One moment." The sounds of chaos in the courtroom evaporated. "There. That will do."

Henry looked up at the octopus with a face dark with anger. "One more piece of stupidity, Judge, and I'm going to end this dream. I know how to do it."

"I have no doubt," answered the judge. "But what if, instead of being in your dream, you are in one of our dreams?"

"Well, I..." Henry scratched his head. "I don't know. I just know that this is my dream. I can't tell you how I know, except that every time I wake up I'm someone else. I mean, Stephen Crane and Lewis Carroll never heard of Henry Fleming or The Last War. They lived a hundred and fifty years ago. You see, right now doesn't even exist. In fact, your honor, it never did."

"I see. And you say that every time you wake up you are someone else?"

"Yes."

"How can you say that you are asleep, then? You may very well be someone else dreaming who wakes up as Henry Fleming. Answer that."

"How can anyone know if he is asleep or awake, or even if he exists?"

"I stink," said Murray Slime. "Therefore, I am." The defense attorney was all over the bench.

"Murray," asked the judge, "what are you doing here?"

"The whisper session was going on so long that I had to find out what you guys were talking about or dry up. Incidentally, I'd like to explore this fellow's line of defense. If my client doesn't exist, then he didn't do it."

"By the same token, Murray, if your client doesn't exist, then neither do you, thus making it impossible to make a motion considering this aspect of your client's materiality. Even should you manage to overcome this difficulty and make your motion on behalf of your client, there will be no one here to hear it, since I, as well, will not exist. And if I do not exist, I refuse to rule on your client's existence one way or the other."

Henry bit his lower lip, scowled, and nodded his head in a measured rhythm. "Just keep it up. Everybody just keep it up and I will evaporate the lot of you."

Koontz Belly sloshed up to the bench. "I say, is this a private conversation, or can anyone join in?"

"Private," said Murray Slime.

"It doesn't matter," said Judge Blechstone.

"I don't care," answered Henry. "In another second or two all of us will inhabit nothingness. I will be awake and everybody else—all of you—will no longer exist."

"That's immaterial," said Belly. "However, I don't think I'm insured for that."

The judge waved a tentacle. "*Can* one be insured for that? Who, for example, could be the beneficiary?"

"Just keep it up," menaced Henry. "Just keep it up."

"Excuse me?" Hugo Pissov was on his feet, waving an arm. "Shouldn't I be up there, too? Everyone else is."

"Please do," offered the judge.

Hugo walked around the defense table and came to a stop

next to Henry. "What's the matter, Henry? You don't look so good."

"It's all right. I don't exist anyway."

"Gyro Gearloose," the metal man confided to Judge Blechstone. "The boy has a few circuits scrambled. I think he was hit by lightning not so long ago."

"Who was fighting Tonto?"

The voice came from behind the youth. He turned to see the huge bloody, pulsing, twitching mass of the King of Hearts. "That's it," said Henry. "I've had it. Does anyone have a pencil?" A blind seer held out a cup. Henry took a pencil from the cup. "Thanks."

"What about a small donation?"

"Sue me in the next dimension."

Henry stooped to waist height and marked a large cross saltire upon the front of Judge Blechstone's bench. He stepped back a few paces and held up a hand for silence. "Farewell one, farewell all." He looked at Hugo. "If you should ever get out of this mess, find my Ma and tell her that I love her." He wondered for a second if he should leave a message for Anne Droid, but he thought better of it. Bending over, he ran at full speed and rammed his head into the judge's bench.

"Ow!" Things went dark for Henry, which no one would dispute.

THIRTY-ONE

Technology Is
Skin Deep

HENRY Was afraid to open his eyes. Malleable reality had so many possibilities. Also he had never personally witnessed a case where the phrase "It can't get worse" had even the slightest element of truth. The universe seemed to be jogging in a regular pattern, which may or may not be a good sign, he opined silently. Something hard, cold, and greasy grasped his hands and shook them as they squeezed.

"I can't possibly express to you my gratitude for all you have done for me."

The youth momentarily entertained a fantasy that he was in control of his appearance in existence. As long as he kept his eyes shut, he believed, the monsters couldn't get him. However, something hard and pain inducing was enthusiastically kneading his hands.

Henry opened an eye. Two things immediately filled his awareness. First, he was riding in a hammock suspended in a compartment of some sort of huge covered wagon. He could hear voices coming from another compartment, and more sounds of heavy breathing and rocks being crushed coming from outside. A few of the sewn-together skins covering the wagon appeared to be still alive. Second, he had a headache that could spawn at least nineteen hundred devils.

He directed his open eye to look downward a bit and saw what it was that was holding his hands. "Hugo." He closed his eye.

"Brother Fleming, I can't tell you how good it is to have you back among the living."

"Let go of my hands."

"Sorry. I was just concerned."

"Unh." Henry flexed his fingers as he pulled himself up on one elbow and looked around at the inside of the compartment. Something dark brown was bubbling in a breaker on a tiny stove. It smelled like the kind of place where dentists would gather on their day off. There were shelves filled with bottles of every color, size, and shape. He leaned closer to the shelf nearest him. The labels he could make out sounded like the menu at Baluga Lou's. There was Toejam, Bellybutton Treasures, Extract of Abcess, Flea Eyebrows, Peanut Butter and Mountain Oysters, Tincture of Eyeball Squeezings, Pickled Hands of Glory, Stew of Boiled Babies (unbaptized), Rat Milk Yogurt, Cat Brain Cheese, Toad Parts (assorted), Powdered Goat Bones, Wizard's Semen, Bat's Blood, Nutrasweet ™, and countless others.

"Where are we?"

"Thanks to you, brother, we're on our way to Mt. Catastrophe to save the world for democracy."

Henry studied the metal man for a long time before he spoke. When he finally did speak, his words were cold. "In my heart of hearts, Hugo, I have this suspicion that what you want to see happen to the world is a lot closer to Sparky's goals than to mine."

Hugo held up his hands. "No. Not at all, brother. I'd be lying if I said that I didn't think robots would do a whole lot better at running this world than humans, but I'm talking about *our* robots, not alien ones. I certainly don't want some bug-eyed 'bot telling me what to do."

"You're bug-eyed."

"Don't be petulant. You know what I mean."

Henry sat up and the pain in his head threatened to send

his brain skittering off into the corner for safety. "Oh, this head. What happened?"

"Don't you remember running into the judge's bench?"

"Yes. That I remember."

"Well, you died."

"How could I have died? It was just a bump on the head. It was supposed to wake me up. Besides, if I died, how come you and I are having this conversation?"

"The doctor revived you. An absolute wizard, Grunt Buggely, even if he is a flaky little creep. This is his wagon."

"How did you get off, Hugo? The last I saw, you were about to be disassembled for slicing off a hunk of the queen's dignity."

"I was innocent, but that wouldn't have been enough without your testimony."

"I don't understand."

"You see, Brother Fleming, 'ought to be guilty' is one of the possible verdicts. It's practically the same thing as a guilty verdict, but the court grants you a moral victory, if not the continued use of your head."

"Explain about the use of— Is beheading the form of execution?"

"Yes. And you saved me from that. Your testimony won me a verdict of 'ought to be not guilty.' That way the court grants you your freedom but reserves the moral victory for someone else."

"How did my testimony—what *was* my testimony?" Henry gingerly touched the lump on the top of his head. "Ow! This headache is making everything fuzzy. I don't remember much about it." The fact was that Henry could remember nothing about it.

Hugo went to the tiny stove and removed the beaker. "I forgot. Grunt Buggely said to give you this when you awakened. It's for the headache."

Henry eyed the dark liquid in the container as the labels on Grunt Buggely's bottles and jars scrolled in the back of his head. "I don't know, Hugo. It seems—"

Hugo grabbed Henry's nose with two fingers and poured the brew down the lad's throat. The youth gagged, reality strobed in and out a few times, he reached past Andromeda and found that the background noise from the Big Bang could be taken care of by switching on the universe's Dolby, and the headache was gone. "Hugo, that stuff is fantastic. My head—" Henry picked something out from between his teeth. It appeared to be a human fingernail. He flicked the paring onto the floor and refused to think upon it anymore.

"What about the trial?"

Hugo resumed his seat upon an ancient leather chest. "Brother, you were terrific. I don't think there was a critter in the entire court that wasn't convinced you hated me."

"No kidding?"

The robot flashed his video sensors and slapped his own knee with a clang. "When I think of the things you said."

"Like what?"

"Oh, that I'm an addict, that I'm a child molester, a communist, a murderer—that was the best part. By the way, how did you ever find out about Adolph Schwartz?"

"You told me after the battle at Keynesburg General. There wasn't anything said that wasn't true. Was there anything else? Did I say more?"

"I should say so. I guess you testified that I had done just about every despicable thing in the world except spark your mother. That's what saved me, brother. They figured that a character as corrupt as mine ought to be innocent."

"My Ma?"

"Sure. I was certain you'd accuse me of throwing the old overdrive to her, but that one you missed."

Henry had a vague recollection of his mother being dragged off by the paddyrollerbots and Hugo crying, "Scarlett, mah honey." Henry grabbed the robot by his throat and squeezed. "Hugo, have you been sparking my Ma?"

"Look at what you're doing." Hugo pointed at his own neck. "I don't use air. What's the matter with you?"

A door opened in the rear of the compartment and General Malaise peeked in. "I heard the commotion and came to see if everything is all right." He nodded at Henry. "You're looking better."

Henry removed his hands from Hugo's neck and held them to the sides of his head. That was when he noticed something peculiar. "What's this safety pin doing stuck through my ear?"

"A free cosmetic touch," answered the general as he came all of the way into the compartment. "Grunt Buggely gave you a good one, too. It's really rusty."

He motioned behind him and several things came into the compartment. There were human arms on crabs, a hedgehog with human ears, a snake with one human foot at the end of its tail, and several others of a similar ilk. It was as though there had been a lackluster sorting job done after a really terrible accident between a troop train and a circus train. "These are my troops. With them we can man the controls at Mt. Catastrophe and take back the government. Then we take back the world!" His men applauded and cheered by growling, clicking, hissing, braying, honking, bracking, and mooing.

Henry stared at them all. "How was the lobster?" he asked with venom.

The crab with the human arms blushed first, which was hard to do. The increased reddish hue washed over them. "We're trying to put that episode behind us, son."

The wagon felt as though it was lurching to a halt. Angry voices from outside could be heard followed by the slam of the wagon's outside door. A small green monster with bug-eyes, pointy white teeth, and long spindly arms and legs entered Henry's compartment and hissed, "We've hit Pennsylvania's Lancaster County line, and the Punk Amish-Quakers won't let us pass if we have any modern machinery aboard. They're getting real ugly, too."

"Ugly?" asked Henry. "What do you mean?"

The monster looked up at him and disjointed his jaw with a crooked smile. "Have you ever seen anyone with a pitchfork stuck through his tongue?"

"That does sound ugly."

General Malaise held out his flappers. "Grunt Buggely, we have no modern machinery. That's why we took the mole wagons for the trip."

Doctor Buggely pointed at Hugo. "What about high tech in low life here?"

The general walked over to Hugo, rapped on the robot's

head twice, and turned to face the doctor. "Can't you turn him into something else? I remember when you turned the King and Queen of Clubs into Hearts."

"Biological organisms are easy. Scrap iron is something else."

Hugo rose to his full height, which was triple that of Grunt Buggely's, even without his neck telescoped. "I am made of the finest Russian stainless steel." He poked the monster with his finger. "You just watch who you're calling scrap iron, wartface."

"I guess," said the doctor, "this is what they mean by a sensitive instrument."

"Hold it," said Henry as he crawled down from his hammock. His eyes went out of focus and his legs were unsteady so he reached out a hand for support. The nearest thing was Grunt Buggely's shoulder, and he grabbed it. Immediately he felt a quivering, slithering beneath his fingers. When he could again focus, the doctor's entire epidermis was cowering on the ankle and foot opposite the shoulder Henry was holding. Since what he was holding was exposed sinew and muscle, Henry released the shoulder.

"Yuck!"

There was a scowl upon Grunt Buggely's face as his skin made a hesitating voyage back to its original position. He said to Henry, "You make my skin crawl."

"Okay, okay." Henry did a slow count to ten. "Now, I can't afford to run into any more walls, so everyone is going to have to cooperate in keeping down the silly level. Now, what is the problem with changing Hugo?"

"I can change him into lead. I can change him into silver, gold, titanium, or any other metal. But the Punk Amish-Quakers don't care what he's made of; they object to what he is."

"Well, what wouldn't they object to? I mean they must use some kind of machinery."

"Like what?"

"Like the wheel. Like . . . bird cages—I don't know. Napoleon's thumb, why don't you *ask* them what their definitions are?"

Grunt Buggely shook his head. "Young Fleming, these

guys don't even use safety pins in their ears. Nothing but old square iron nails, an occasional wood chisel or screwdriver. Bah! Religious fanatics."

Henry pursed his lips and touched Grunt Buggely's shoulder again with a single fingertip. Again the monster's epidermis cowered upon the opposite ankle. "Hmmm." He touched the kneecap above the ankle, thus causing the skin to scoot off Grunt Buggely's foot altogether. As the organ skittered across the floor, Henry motioned with his hands. "Come on, surround it. Keep Hugo inside the circle."

In moments there was a circle around Grunt Buggely's epidermis and the metal man. As the circle was made tighter and tighter, the two were forced closer and closer together. At one point the skin grew a mouth full of fangs and growled at Hugo. Then, as General Malaise reached out a flapper, the skin leaped upon the metal man and gathered at the top of his head. Henry gestured and the circle opened slightly, allowing the epidermis to flow slowly all over Hugo's body. "There," said Henry smugly. "Bring on the inspectors."

"This is embarrassing," said Grunt Buggely as he rummaged through the leather chest Hugo had been using for a seat. "There must be something in here that I can wear."

The chest appeared to cough, and Henry noticed the head, arms, legs, and the rest of the body to which it was attached. It made up the wagon itself. The chest coughed again and the doctor said, "I told you to stop smoking." He pulled a herringbone alligator suit out of the chest and slammed it shut.

"Henry," called Hugo, a touch of fear and trepidation in his voice. "This thing that is all over me is singing."

"Don't tell me the song's title,"* offered Henry, "and I'll get you all of the Addix you'll ever want."

*I just can't bear to put it in print. For those who can't figure this one out, write the author c/o the publisher.

THIRTY-TWO

Friendly Persuasion

AS Henry stepped down from the wagon, he saw that it was as long as a railiner car and was being pulled by a team of twenty giant moles. In the tunnel, in front of the team, was a roadblock. In front of the roadblock was a gang brandishing chains, pitchforks, torches, two-handed saws, and scrub brushes. The obvious leader of the gang was tall, rawboned, and sported a beard with no mustache. He wore a broad-brimmed black hat, his beard was shaped into black spikes, and he wore a beaver trap clamped on his left ear. The man addressed Henry. "I am called Vicious Birdwell. Who art thou?"

"I art, uh, am Henry Fleming."

Vicious Birdwell nodded once and let his gaze pass to the others. "Bringest thou into our land any worldly devices? VCRs, PCs, parking meters, indoor plumbing, pay toilets?"

Everybody shook their heads to indicate a negative response. Birdwell gestured with his hand and four of his colleagues parted from the band and entered the wagon to search. "Thou hast come upon the land of Friends, friends, and in service to the Inner Light, we may not allow thee to cross our borders if evil intentions move thee."

He stopped in front of Hugo and pushed back his hat. "Now, what might thee be, friend?"

"I am Hugo Pi—" Hugo coughed. "Just Hugo, friend."

"Thy skin is of an unwholesome color and texture, friend. Art thou infirm?"

"It's this new soap I've been using."

"Nothing perfumed."

"No, of course not. I think it's called Hair Shirt and Ashes."

Vicious Birdwell leaned forward and sniffed at Hugo. Actually he sniffed at Grunt Buggely's skin on Hugo. "Definitely not perfumed." He turned and paused before Dr. Buggely. "I can see thy muscles, friend."

"My people have always been thin-skinned," hissed Grunt Buggely.

"Irish, eh?"

"Erin go bra."

The leader of the gang moved on and paused before General Malaise. "How art thou, friend?"

"Fine." The general saluted with his right flapper.

Vicious Birdwell examined the general's uniform and returned his gaze to Malaise's eyes. "We oppose war. Thou art a part of a great evil. Why we stand and guard this tunnel is due to the work done by thee and thy kind."

"That was a long time ago, Birdwell. Right now I'm trying to save everybody's bacon." One of the general's men oinked enthusiastically at this remark.

The four Punk Amish-Quakers came down from the wagon. Birdwell turned to them and asked, "Friend Scumbucket, are they holding?"

Scumbucket, a portly fellow with a blue beard and several feet of barbed wire coiled through his earlobes, shook his head at Birdwell. "Everything inside is organic and natural, depending upon thy planet of origin, Friend Birdwell."

"Very good." Birdwell faced the travelers. "Then there is only one issue left to resolve: what are thy intentions? Are they warlike and evil, or peaceful and good?"

"Oh, I would say peaceful and good," answered Henry, turning to Hugo. "Wouldn't you?"

"Oh yes, I'd say so. Definitely peaceful and good. Buggely?"

"Hee, hee, yesssss. Peaceful and good, hee, hee, heeeee."

"If thine plans are so beneficent, friend,"—Birdwell fixed the youth with a stare—"Then share them with us."

"All we intend doing is taking over the Mt. Catastrophe Ultimate Retaliation Control Center so we can overthrow the government . . . and threaten to nuke the Russians . . . to force them to call off the competition—I know how it sounds, but it's not like that at all."

"We must seek spiritual guidance as to what to do about this matter. Thee and thy companions will accompany us at our meeting." He gestured to the others. "Put them back on the wagon and lead their team to the meeting house."

Henry saw Friend Scumbucket grin as he crushed a six by six with his bare hands as though it were so much bread.

"I want my skin back," demanded Grunt Buggely. "If I'm to be flayed alive, I'd rather it be with my skin on than off."

"You're such a baby," said Hugo. "Why don't you stop thinking of yourself for half a second and try and figure out how we can get out of this mess."

"I want my skin back."

"Enough," said Henry. He looked at General Malaise. "What will they do if our intentions are found to be evil?"

"No one knows. None of the parties who planned to cross here have ever been heard from again."

Henry's jaw opened as his eyes went wide. "Then why in the name of Hannibal did we come this way?"

"Well, we've gotten some negative reports from those who have used other routes. We haven't gotten *any* negative reports about this route."

"In other words, no reports at all." Henry held his hand to his forehead. "Don't you consider never hearing from anyone who crossed here a big-time negative?"

"Some could look at it that way, I suppose. Just about anything one looks at may be viewed through either a positive or negative attitude. We chose to be positive."

"Great Caesar's ghost." Henry faced Dr. Buggely. "What about you? You're supposed to be a wizard."

"Gee, fella, thanks a heap. Why don't you stick your head outside and announce it to every pitchfork-wielding fruitcake under Pennsylvania? What do you think those gooseberries out there are going to do to me if they find out I can do a little magic? Have you ever been burned up in a wicker basket?"

"Druids," interrupted Henry. "Druids did the thing with the baskets, not Punk Amish-Quakers."

"Who cares!" hissed the monster. "Man, I even look like something that needs to be exorcised out of someone. When they get their hooks into me—"

"By Alcibiades's bald spot, what is the point of having this dream if all I can come up with in the way of a wizard is a stretched-out toad with no imagination and a paranoia problem? We need Merlin, Glenda the Good, someone with clout!"

"Just you wait one minute, Henry Fleming!" Grunt Buggely stabbed a naked finger into Henry's breadbasket. "If it wasn't for my so-called magic, you'd be dead right now. That took a bit of real wizardry, I can tell you."

"Wait." Hugo held up a hand. Grunt Buggely's skin slid down and hung loose from the robot's elbow. "I've been searching through some old programs. I have an idea and it just might work." He put his arm around Grunt Buggely and led him away saying, "I think I can get you your skin back, *and* get us out of this fix. Maybe I can drum up some additional help to take over Mt. Catastrophe. All you need to do is that voodoo that you do so well."

"Who do?"

"You do."

And the pair faded into the wizard's laboratory to prepare for the coming. . . .

THIRTY-THREE

The Incarnation of Krishna Pissov

HUGO And the wizard spent the remainder of the trip locked in Buggely's laboratory. At odd moments strange sounds and smells would emerge, but the pair kept their own counsel. When the wagon halted and Scumbucket came to escort them to the meeting, only then did the laboratory door open. Neither the abbreviated monster nor the skin-covered robot looked any different, save for a touch of smugness.

The meeting hall was silent and divided down its long axis by a spiked barrier. On either side of the barrier were benches stepped such that the farther one sat from the barrier, the higher one sat. Men sat on one side, women on the other. Hugo, Grunt Buggely, and Henry sat near the front of the men's side and General Malaise and the male members of his force sat behind them. All of the men, including our adventurers, wore hats. Even if it wasn't a Mithraeum, thought Henry, it was still a house of worship.

The Punk Amish-Quaker women were a brutal-looking lot. The current fashion appeared to be to use wooden potato mashers inserted through the depressor alae nasi in place of a nose ring or nose bone. Their hair was dyed deep pokeberry purple and was curled, spiked, and shaped with laundry starch. Each hairdo was surmounted by a tiny gray bonnet. Their dresses were uniform gray leather miniskirts supported by curried hairy legs. It wasn't just that the legs were unshaven, Henry observed. That hadn't been in fashion among women since before The War. These women, however, looked as though they were wearing sheepskin chaps. The children were sneaking around attaching "666, Denounce Me" signs on unsuspecting backsides.

Grunt Buggely and Hugo were snickering, and Henry shooshed them. After a very long stretch of this silence, Vicious Birdwell, sitting to their right, got to his feet. "I guarded the eastern tunnel today, and I would like to bear witness to Revelation, chapter sixteen, verses thirteen and fourteen: 'And I saw three unclean spirits like frogs—'"

"Who looks like a frog?" demanded the general.

"Shhhhh!" shooshed Grunt Buggely.

"I thank thee, Friend Buggely," said Vicious. He bushed up his eyebrows and resumed. "'And I saw three unclean spirits like frogs come out of the mouth of the dragon, and out of the mouth of the beast, and out of the mouth of the false prophet.'" Birdwell glared down at Buggely, Hugo, the general, and Henry. He lifted an outstretched finger that trembled with passion. "'For they are the spirits of devils, working miracles, which go forth unto the kings of the earth and of the whole world, to gather them to the battle of that great day of God Almighty.'"

"Amen, Friend Birdwell," croaked a slathering fanged creature from the women's side.

Birdwell resumed his place on the bench, and silence again filled the room. On the women's side a girl with pimples the size of golf balls stood up and said, "I made a chocolate cake last night and I would like to thank God for how well it came out." She sat down and immediately sprang back to her feet. "I ate an entire chocolate cake last night, and I want to thank God for how well it tasted." She sat down and immediately sprang back to her feet. "I got sick on chocolate cake last night, and I would like to ask God to forgive my gluttony." She sat down and immediately sprang back to her feet. "I plan to make an angelfood cake tonight, and I want to ask God to inspire my efforts." She sat down and seemed to drift off into a sugared dreamland.

After a nerve-racking stretch of silence, Henry got to his feet. "I don't think I'm evil. Ever since I joined the Economy I've only tried to do the right thing. That's all I'm trying to do now. That's all any of us are trying to do. We don't want war. All we want to do is to take the government back from an alien power. If you want to see evil, you should check out the robot called Sparky that's going to wind up in control of everything unless we do something." Henry sat down, folded his arms, and crossed his legs. Even if it was only a dream, he felt very discouraged.

After more silence, one of the men who Henry didn't know got to his feet and said with a deathly calm, "It looks like we'll have to burn 'em at the stake. Our oxygen ration is short this month, so we'll have to use electric instead of wood."

Henry punched General Malaise in the shoulder. "Aren't you going to say anything? They're planning on killing us."

All the general could do was weep.

One of the women stood up. "I don't think it's God's will to burn these folks with electric." She looked slightly offended at the tiny round of applause her sentiment drew from Henry, the general and his troops. "As I said, I don't think God wants electric. That's why He gave us the gift of wood."

"Great," muttered Henry.

After a period of silence, Friend Scumbucket got to his feet. "Out of the past five hundred demons, devils, heretics, and evildoers we have burned, thirty-one percent went by wood, twenty-three by coal, seven by gas, nine by oil, eleven by nuclear, and nineteen by electric. For electric, that's twelve percent by electric heat and seven percent by the direct application method. The highest percentage of those who repented before being consumed was by the direct application electric method."

The woman who favored wood got to her feet. "Vernon Scumbucket, I don't hold with thy reformed ways. I've said it before and I'll say it again: electric is newfangled, modern, too worldly. That goes for gas, oil, and nuclear, too. I'm willing to bend a bit for coal, but that's as far as I'm willing to go. Wood is best, as thee knowest damned well, and that's that."

Scumbucket and the woman resumed their seats and all awaited in silence for the Inner Light to resolve the many issues before the meeting.

"Ahem."

Henry looked for the source of the tiny voice and saw Grunt Buggely standing on his bench, his hat pushed far enough back on his head so that he could see. "I am a visitor at thy meeting, friends, and this is a moment when the fate of God's universe hinges upon what thou doest next, hee, hee, heeee." The monster's bugged eyes looked slyly at Hugo, then he faced the assembly. "I bear witness to Revelation, chapter one, verses twelve through eighteen. 'And I turned to see the voice that spake with me. And being turned I saw seven golden candlesticks.'"

Henry saw six brass cylinders, three on either side of Hugo, telescope up from the floor at the same time as Grunt Buggely's skin began falling from the uppermost parts of the robot, revealing glowing gold plating and a magnesium-white wig. His video sensors had been replaced with high-wattage bulbs that lit up the meeting room. Hugo still had his Confederate general's uniform on, but the yellow sash was wrapped around his upper chest. A golden tassel hung out of his mouth. Everyone in the meeting room cowered at the spectacle.

"'And in the midst of the seven candlesticks,'" resumed the monster, "'*one* like unto the Son of man, clothed with a garment down to the foot, and girt about the paps with a golden girdle. His head and his hairs '"—Buggely pointed toward the wig—"'were white like wool, as white as snow; and his eyes'"—the wizard pointed at Hugo's new video sensors—"'were as a flame of fire.'" Buggely pointed at Hugo's feet, newly plated as well. "'And his feet like unto fine brass, as if they burned in a furnace; and his voice'"—Hugo's synthesizer cranked up the noise slide—"'as the sound of many waters.'"

Hugo touched off a bunch of sparklers and held them in his right hand as he began pulling his cavalry saber out of his mouth with his left hand. Grunt Buggely continued the narrative.

"'And he had in his right hand,' hee, hee, heeee, 'seven stars; and out of his mouth went a sharp two edged sword; and his countenance was as the sun shineth in his strength.'"

Grunt Buggely fell at Hugo's feet and tried to catch his skin as the robot laid the hand with the burnt-out sparklers in it upon the monster and said unto him, "'Fear not; I am the first and the last: I am he that liveth, and was dead, and, behold, I am alive for evermore, Amen; and have the keys of hell and of death.'"

Henry shook his head in disgust and said, "Jesus Christ."

"Eggzacktly!" screamed the assembly.

Later, as Vicious Birdwell's army assembled in mole-powered vehicles behind Buggely's twenty-mole-team wagon, Hugo grouchoed his magnesium eyebrows at Henry. "Well, Brother Fleming? Was that a solution, or was that a solution? You didn't know I used to sell Bibles, did you?"

"You think you're so smart," sneered Henry as he climbed into the wagon. "You were supposed to have a two-edged sword in your mouth. A cavalry saber is a single-edged weapon. Everybody knows that."

"Bless you, my son," said Hugo as he followed Henry into the wagon, waving at the observing faithful as he did so. "Bless you. Bless you, all. Dominoes fo' mo' biscuts." Grunt Buggely scooted past in hot pursuit of his birthday suit.

They stocked the wagons with provisions, and they were required by local law and custom to purchase their pies and pastries from Vicious Birdwell's in-laws, a pair of sisters whose brother's son, Nasty Penn, made the deliveries. Nasty delivered a shoofly pie, an apple pie, and a gooseberry pie. Along with the pies, he presented a bill for sixty dollars. General Malaise took delivery, and after he had paid Nasty Penn, he looked at the receipt and said to Henry, "Have you seen the pie rates of Penn's aunts?"

THIRTY-FOUR

Through the Liquor Glass

AS The wagon train rolled west along Sub I-70, Henry slept several times. None of these slumbers, however, brought him back to either Stephen Crane's world or to Lewis Carroll's world, nor to any other. He puzzled over this for many days, until he at last accepted that the reality into which he had been born was indeed the same one in which he would die.

He had been dreaming when he had thought he was Crane and Carroll. Still, there was a nagging suspicion in the back of his head that things were hardly ever as they appeared to be, and perhaps, at any time, reality might do another bait-and-switch on him. These things were heavy on his mind as the wagon train crossed beneath the Columbus Wastes. Not far to the north was Keynesburg and where he had first met the truth about the Economy, and about himself.

"I have come an awfully long way to wind up where I began," he reflected. Voices came from the Peace Room —what they now called the large rear compartment on Buggely's wagon. In there General Malaise, his men, Hugo, Grunt Buggely, Vicious Birdwell, and his lieutenants were planning out the details for the assault on Mt. Catastrophe.

There would be a battle. On Henry's mind, however, was the memory of his flight before the scabdroids at Keynesburg General. Would he run again? He felt very alone. He wished that he had someone at his side to listen to his troubles and to tell him that everything would turn out all right.

Alone with his thoughts, Henry was poking around the wizard's laboratory when he came across a box containing an ancient manuscript and a strangely shaped piece of black glass. Opening the volume, the youth could see that much of the book was written in an undecipherable script. Here and there, however, translations had been written into the margins. One such translation that he could easily read said, "Look at this glass eating lemon zest, And then see the one that you love best."

"Now, where would I find lemon zest?" asked the youth.

Upon the glass appeared the inscription: "Left wall, middle shelf, the blue jar near the right." Henry stared in wonder at the inscription. He looked at the left wall, middle shelf, and near the right he saw a blue jar labeled Lemon Zest, right between a white jar labeled Lemming Sperm and a yellow jar labeled Lemur Snot.

"It pays to read labels carefully," observed the youth as he took down the blue jar. He opened the top and the heady smell of lemon filled the compartment.

He took a pinch of the coarse yellow powder inside the jar and placed it upon his tongue as he looked at the piece of black glass. Coils of yellow and orange fire turned in the glass, finally resolving into the image of Anne Droid.

"Anne!" The name was torn from his lips by involuntary passion.

"Hi, John," answered the image.

"Anne, I miss you so." There, thought the youth. I have said it. I have admitted it to myself. I don't care if it makes me a mechanisexual. I love her.

"Anne, if I could only have you with me."

The image of Anne Droid put her thumbs in the waistband of her net panties and slowly moved her thumbs back and forth around her waist. "Just turn the page, John."

Henry glanced at Grunt Buggely's ancient manuscript, and back at the glass, but the image was gone. "The book? Did you mean—don't go!"

Quickly Henry returned to the manuscript and turned the page. The handwritten translation said, "To have your love here in your arm, This ancient draught should be your charm: Blackghast fungus boiled up, The broth poured straight into a cup; Salt it down with witch's sand, Then spice it up with a baboon's gland; Drink it down, and then this last: Jump in bed and have a blast."

The youth searched among the shelves until he found the Blackghast fungus. He opened the black iron container and took a whiff. "Great Alexander's sneakers, that's stiff."

He took a piece, dropped it into a beaker of Boiler Stuff that smelled like varnish remover. Placing the beaker on the tiny stove, he searched for and found the witch's sand as well as the pickled baboon's testicle.

When the fungus looked as though whatever power it had in it had been boiled out, Henry poured the broth into a mug and put several pinches of witch's sand into it. The fluid within boiled again with an icy green light. Eyes could be seen peeking out between the coils of clouds above the container, and just as the bottom of the mug began growing spider legs, the brew calmed and acquired a blue hue.

The youth grimaced as he held the pickled monkey nut over the liquid. "This is it." He dropped it in and watched as it dissolved, changing the liquid's blue hue to amber. Henry lifted the mug and sniffed at it. "It smells like Jack Daniel's." He shrugged and quaffed it with one huge gulp.

He coughed, every particle of reality exchanged places with every other particle of reality, and he watched as his own head rotated on his shoulders three times. As the world feathered back into sync with the universe, Henry managed to focus on the black glass. He waited for whatever to happen, but it just didn't.

"Oh," he remembered, "I was supposed to get into bed."

He turned around and there in all of her splendor spread out upon the bed was the well-turned perfection of Anne Droid. Her actual presence startled Henry so much that he fell backward. Placing a hand behind him to soften his fall, his fingers touched the black glass and he fell through it into a world of dark.

"Dammit," cursed the youth as he tumbled ever downward through the sulfurous fumes. "Not again!"

THIRTY-FIVE

Dis Ain't No City

AS If in a dream, Henry awakened walking the banks of a great river. He could tell it was very wide by the reflection of the flames and the distant sounds of screaming coming from the other side. There were sounds of screaming on his side of the river, too. There were hills of tortured bodies screaming in agony. He closed his eyes against the sights, turned from the sounds, and entered a dense fog filled with black air.

"Where am I?" he cried. "Hey! Can anyone tell me where I am?"

Aside from the screams and the brush of the fog, there were no sounds except a jingle tune that seemed to be played on a child's toy piano. Henry stumbled toward the sound until, suddenly, three horrors rose up in front of him. They were bloodstained and had human arms, but they wore green hydra-skin belts. For hair they had serpents, and one of the horrors was teasing her snakes.

"A gracious good morning," said the center horror with a nasal voice that seemed somehow oddly familiar. "We are the City of Dis Information. May we help you?"

"Disinformation?"

The three horrors cackled. "No, you foolish thing. That's City of Dis (space) Information. May we help you?"

Henry scratched his head. "I don't know if anyone can help me."

"You sound discouraged."

He smiled bitterly. "I guess I am. Maybe I should sell my soul—"

Immediately there was a red fellow with goat legs, a pointed tail, and horns holding a piece of paper in front of him. The red one pulled out a Bic and clicked it. "Just sign here."

"I was just joking." Henry looked at the form. It appeared to be a contract of some sort. "What's it for?"

"Anything you want."

"What's it going to cost?"

"Your soul."

"Hmmm." Henry examined the document but was interrupted by one of the three horrors.

"I'm sorry, sir, but we must get on with our other customers. Can we help you?"

The one with the horns looked angrily at the three sisters. "We're right in the middle of something. Can he get back to you later?"

"Don't be absurd, goat legs." She cackled and snorted, "You little devil, you." She laughed some more and turned to Henry. "Okay, kid. What information do you want?"

Henry handed the document back to the red fellow with the horns. "I don't think so. The last time I signed one of these things it didn't turn out anything like I thought it would." He turned back to the horror. "This is the City of Dis?"

"That's right. Where do you want to go? There are lots of attractions. Maybe you'd like to check out some of the hot spots the regular tourists don't see."

"Hot spots!" cackled the horror who was teasing her snakes.

"Now who's the little devil?" cackled the third horror.

When the first horror could bring herself to stop laughing, she dried her bloodshot eyes and addressed the youth. "Perhaps you read our brochure?" She held out a fairly thick oversized book.

Henry took it and read the title. "What's a divine comedy?"

"Don't worry about it," cackled the second horror. "Just get a load of the pictures!" The three horrors fell all over themselves, they were laughing so hard.

Henry glanced through the pictures and saw nothing but one horror after another. Bodies and mere pieces of bodies in torment. There were flames, ice, brimstone, and all the latest tortures. Then he saw a face that he recognized. It was a nude drawing of a man, his face contorted in agony. "That's Stephen Crane."

"Yes," cackled the central horror. "Would you like to meet him?"

"Where would he be?" the youth asked cautiously.

The horror flipped a Rolodex. "Tha-a-a-a-a-t's the Eighth Circle." She ran a fingertip down the card. "Ninth—no, Tenth Pouch."

"How do I get there?"

"Repeat after me," said the center horror. "There's no place like home. There's no place like . . ."

"There's no place like home," Henry repeated. "There's n—"

"Oh, goodness gracious, what a silly pudding you are!" The three horrors laughed. "It was a joke, diddle-brain."

Henry's face grew hot. "Look—"

The central horror touched him with a magic wand and, poof, he was once again zipping through misty layers of improbability.

THIRTY-SIX

Waiting for Vergil

THE Youth found himself seated at a table. He still had on his VMI costume, which set him apart from the others, who were all quite naked.

Directly across the table from Henry was Stephen Crane. Behind him the constantly writhing shadows were tinged with red and orange flames belching from mighty furnaces. There was a distinct smell of sulfur in the air. In addition, it was rather warm.

Henry looked back at Crane's tormented face. Crane was trying to decide between calling or folding his hand. The only other person left in the hand was seated to Henry's right. He was a portly chap wearing only a short mustache. He looked over his glasses at Stephen Crane. "Are you planning on playing those cards, or playing with them?"

Crane, also quite naked, held his hand very close to his face and squeezed them into a fan one at a time. He picked up five of the golden chips and tossed them in the middle of the table. "I think you're bluffing, George. I call your fifty years and"—he threw ten more golden chips on the pile—"raise you a hundred."

As the one called George looked back at his hand to review its contents, Henry looked at the naked man on his left. "Why, you're Frank Baum, aren't you?"

The man smiled pleasantly. "Why, yes I am. Have we met before?"

"Once. Some time ago back when I was Stephen Crane for a bit. We had a discussion about Tick Tock and mince pie."

"I'm terribly sorry, but I don't recall."

"It's probably not important." Henry stuck his finger in the collar of his VMI uniform blouse. "Doesn't it seem a little warm in here to you?"

"Quite. I'm pleased to see you back."

"That doesn't seem odd to you, Mr. Baum?"

"Odd? What seems odd?"

"That I used to be Stephen Crane?"

The man shook his head. "No. Nothing is odd here. Everything is not only possible, it's probable."

"Will you two shut up," grumped George. "You make it impossible to think with all your chatter."

"Sorry, George," said Baum. He pushed his chair back from the table and indicated to Henry to do the same. Once the youth had his chair back, Baum whispered into his ear. "That fellow to your right is H. G. Wells. Next to him—"

"I know him," Henry whispered back. "That's Lewis Carroll."

"His real name is Charles Dodgson. We call him Chuck. It really pisses him. Of course you know Stephen Crane, having been him for a time."

"Yes. I don't know that older gentleman sleeping in the chair between you and Mr. Crane, though."

"Jules Verne—"

Bam! Stephen Crane slammed his hand down in front of Verne. "Wake up, Jules! You're dribbling again."

"Pardon." The man with the white beard pulled a handkerchief out of thin air and dabbed at his facial hair.

Crane looked over his cards at Wells. "That's a hundred years to you, George."

"I wish I'd never said those nice things about your story."

" 'The Open Boat'?"

"Of course. Dreary thing."

Crane leaned back in his chair and placed his hand face down on the table. "Are you going to play those cards, George, or play with them?"

"Just a minute." Wells shook his head as he studied his cards. "I wish I had a cigar right now. I can't believe that we're not allowed to smoke down here—especially down here."

"The devil is evil," said Jules. "He's not stupid."

George threw his hand into the discard pile. "Damn. What did you have, Stephen?"

"Don't be an idiot," Crane shoved his hand into the discards. "You have to pay to see them." He nodded at Henry. "You must be one of those modern authors. Very glad to see you here. What have you written?"

"I haven't written anything."

"Is this a transparent stab at modesty?"

"I don't know what you mean."

Crane pointed his thumb at Chuck. "Now, some might say that Chuck hasn't written anything."

Henry shook his head. "No, he's Lewis Carroll. He wrote *Alice's Adventures in Wonderland*."

There were dirty chuckles from everyone at the table save Chuck Dodgson. George jabbed Chuck in the ribs with his elbow, causing the Oxford don to flush red all over.

"Whatever you've written," said Crane, "you're welcome. Personally, I hate five-handed poker. It screws up all of the odds." As Crane raked in his chips, he shoved the cards at Baum. "Your deal, Frank."

Baum shuffled the cards and slapped them down at Henry's left elbow. "Cut."

"Is there any way out of here? I have something rather important to do."

Baum tapped on the deck. "Cut."

Henry removed a few cards from the top and Baum gathered up the deck and began the deal. A pile of golden chips magically appeared in front of Henry. He held one of the chips and read it. It said: "ten years' ind."

"Stephen has the power," said Baum as he finished dealing the one down and one up for stud. Crane's visible card was the king of clubs. Henry had the nine of diamonds and he noticed that one of the nines, the club, was face up in front of Baum.

Crane checked his hole card and threw a chip into the center of the table. As Lewis Carroll, who had a queen up, examined his hole card, Crane looked at Henry. "Where're you from, kid?"

"Originally Ft. Calley, Texas. More recently I was traveling west under Ohio. Could you tell me where this is?"

Carroll bumped it ten years and H. G. Wells chuckled as he threw in two chips. "I take it you never studied much."

"I guess not—"

Wells pointed at Henry's nine. "It's twenty to you."

"What's that mean, ten years' ind.?"

"Ten years' indulgence."

"What's that?"

"That's ten years off your sentence down here. Go ahead. Bet or fold."

Henry looked at his hole card: the ten of clubs. He tossed in two chips. Baum folded and Henry asked him, "Where is this?"

"Just one of many, many realities." Baum looked across the table at Dodgson. "I keep getting the pouches, places, and circles all mixed up."

Chuck placed the queen of hearts neatly over his hole card. "This is the Tenth Pouch of the Eighth Circle. Considering when he lived, I think Dante was very imaginative."

"Imaginative?"

"Yes."

"He was a plagiarist. Everybody knows he stole the entire concept from Augustine's *City of God*."

"Now, there was some top drawer fantasy," said Wells.

"Anyway," said Baum, "I'd certainly like to get my hands on the sonofabitch. How about it, Jules, are you in or out?"

The white-bearded fellow dropped in two chips. "I think I will try another card."

Henry held out his hands. "Where is the Tenth Pouch of the Eighth whatever—"

"Hell," completed George, raising his eyebrows. "You know—Hades, the Infernal Regions."

"This is a special corner for falsifiers of words," Chuck

Dodgson filled in. He smiled ruefully. "Who would have thought that it would apply to fiction writers?"

"Chuck," said George, "you'd be down here roasting in any event. He looked at Crane. "Isn't there a spot kept especially hot for child molesters?"

"I protest!" Dodgson jumped to his feet, remembered what he was wearing, and sat down, bright red all over. "I never did any such thing."

"What about all of those feelthy Franch peectures?" asked Jules.

"Those were nude studies!"

"Uh huh," said Frank. "You know what they say in New York: one man's art is another's eight to ten in Attica."

Dodgson glared at George. "In any event, you certainly have no room to swing accusations, dumping your wife and running off with one of your pimpled students."

"That was my haunting dream of finding sexual perfection with an ideal partner!"

"Sounds like George chasing down all of the loose nookie in Britain to me."

"Cards," called Baum. He turned up a six for Jules, making it a pair, a three for Stephen, giving him a pair of gnarks, a seven for Dodgson which was no improvement, a seven for Wells who promptly folded, and a queen for Henry. Henry looked again at his hole card. It was still a ten of clubs. "You have the pair, Jules."

"How did you all get here?"

Verne stroked his beard. "Let me see." He shrugged and tossed in ten years. Stephen Crane bit his lower lip, shook his head, and folded. As Dodgson contemplated his hole card, Stephen Crane pointed at the Oxford don.

"We were all over at the candy man's place looking at his sicko pictures—"

"Those are nude studies. I find the nude forms of young children very appealing."

"I just bet you do. Anyway, old Hey Little Girl, You Wanna Piece of Candy was showing us this huge black mirror he picked up at an estate auction. George started reading from an old manuscript that Chuck had picked up with the mirror, and the next thing any of us knew, here we were."

Jules chuckled and said, "My journey to the center of the earth."

"That's how I got here," said Henry. "I fell into a piece of black glass."

"Where is it now?" asked Frank.

"Somewhere under Ohio, heading west with Anne Droid, my. . ." All the youth could do was fall silent.

Frank nodded at Chuck. "It's your bet."

Dodgson bumped it ten years and looked at Henry. "Twenty to you."

Henry threw it two chips and Baum started the cards around again. "Jules, you get a five, no help to the pair. Chuck, you get a—another five, no help to anyone, and. . ." He looked at the youth. "You haven't introduced yourself yet."

"Fleming. Henry Fleming."

"How curious," remarked Crane. "I once wrote a story about a boy named Henry Fleming."

"I know. Would you be willing to tell me how the story ended?"

"I would be willing," answered Crane, "but the sad truth is that I simply don't know. There are so many versions, you see."

"Can't you remember the one you wrote?"

"It's very vague. You see, you're the hundred and third story character of ours that's shown up to join our game." He grinned and spoke to Jules. "That Captain Nemo that showed up last time was a bit of a sissy, wasn't he?"

Jules Verne clasped his hands together and looked at Crane through narrowed eyes. "I remember the Henry Fleming before last."

"Okay, I apologize about—"

"That boy tried to rape George, here."

"I apologized, Jules."

"Excuse me," interrupted Henry, "but I really must be going. Could you please tell me how to get out of here."

A round of chuckles circled the table. Stephen Crane motioned with his thumb over his shoulder. "Have you met the guy with the contract?"

"Red suit, bad attitude?"

"That's the one. Sign up and you can get out of here, for a while. Unfortunately, should you sign the contract, when you return it's for ever and ever."

"Amen," said Jules.

"What else?" asked Henry.

Wells held up one of his chips. "Win all of these."

"Win them?"

"That's why we're playing this game. Win all of the chips, and your time's up."

Henry looked around at the table. "I don't get it. There're a lot of chips here, but someone should have won them all by now."

"Look in the shadows behind you."

Henry looked and looked. After his eyes adjusted a bit to the darkness, he could just barely make out a mountain of chips twenty feet high. The youth looked at Baum and tapped on the table. "My card."

"Forgive me. You, Henry my boy, get a nine, making a pair. You have the bet."

Henry threw in twelve chips. "There's the twenty, and I bump a hundred."

Jules's eyebrows arched. "My goodness, has the new boy trips?" He pursed his lips, grabbed some chips, then folded his pair.

Dodgson threw in ten additional chips. "I have to keep you honest, Fleming."

George snickered, "Which is more than anyone ever did for you."

"I've had about enough of you, Wells."

"Panty sniffer."

"Nookie hound."

"Cards," said Frank. "Chuck, you get Henry's nine. And Henry, you get . . ." He put the ace of clubs on Henry's pile. "A big bullet. You still have the bet, Henry."

Dodgson was only staying in because he had a pair of queens, Henry knew. Of course the queens beat Henry's hand, but not from across the table. The trick would be in betting the proper amount. Too little and it wouldn't cost anything, so Dodgson would call. Too much and it would look as though he was trying to appear confident. It would be best to appear confident trying to appear unsure to sucker Dodgson in for another bet, thus making it obvious that he either had trip nines or aces and nines, thus causing the Oxford don to fold.

Henry threw out twenty chips and looked at Chuck. "Two hundred years."

Dodgson wrestled with it for a time, then folded. He reached across the table to look at Henry's hole card. The youth slammed his hand down on his hole card. "No pay, no peek."

"I say." Dodgson sat upright, his curiosity unsatiated. As Jules gathered up the cards, Chuck glanced over his shoulder. "When *is* that man going to show up?"

"Who?" asked Henry.

"Vergil, of course."

"Vergil who?"

George looked at Henry as though the youth were something that had crawled from out of a rotting log. "Vergil *who?*"

"Yes," confirmed Henry. "I never heard of him."

"Publius Vergilius Maro," George clarified. Seeing the blank look on Henry's face, Wells clarified further. "The author of the *Aeneid?*"

"Sorry."

"What is the point of becoming a published author if they forget all about you after a few centuries?"

"When was Vergil Whatshisface alive?"

"First century B.C."

"That's a long time ago." Henry faced Dodgson. "Why are you waiting for him?"

"Surely you have noticed that the one fellow who should be here, Durante Alighieri himself, is absent."

"Who?"

"Dante," explained Baum. "*The Divine Comedy?* The fellow who stole this place from St. Augustine?"

"Jules, wasn't his mother an alcoholic?" asked Stephen.

"Dante's or Augustine's?"

"Either one."

"Augustine's mother, Monica, was in the sauce."

"In any event," Baum said as he reclaimed the floor, "in

the process of designing a hell for fiction writers, he gave himself an out. His ticket out was his guide, the Roman poet Vergil."

"And," said Chuck, "if anyone at all deserves to be down here, it's the poets."

Wells rubbed his chin and leaned back in his chair. "My dear Chuck, what about old 'Twas brillig, and the slithy toves did etcetera, etcetera in the wabe'?"

"'Jabberwocky' was a satire."

"Have you ever noticed," observed Stephen, "that every time a poet or writer puts out a real piece of crap, he calls it a satire or a parody?"

"Nevertheless," said Jules, "I do believe that Dante had the poets condemned to the Ninth Circle, didn't he?"

Chuck Dodgson snorted. "Nice guy, wasn't he? That was a gift for his competition. I notice that he left a neat loophole out of the pit for himself."

"Anyway," reasserted Baum, "we have a theory that, if he returns, Vergil can lead us all out of here."

"How long have you been waiting for him?" inquired the youth.

"It's hard to tell," Wells responded. "There are no clocks or calendars. What year was it where you were?"

"It was 2042."

"Then by now it's been ninety-six years for me," said Wells.

Baum turned to his left. "Deal 'em, Jules. The deck is getting cold."

"Draw, gentlemen."

As the cards went around, Henry wiped the perspiration from his forehead. "I don't see how anyone can just dream up a reality and have it exist. It doesn't make any sense."

"I don't know," said George as he sorted through his cards. "What makes sense is always a moment by moment affair. That fellow Einstein who was through here on his way to the Ninth Circle, Fourth Ring, thought the idea might wash. It's something like the imaginable universes all exist at the same place and time. Movement from one to the other is possible through imagination, dreams, nightmares, what have you."

"Einstein never said that," Baum corrected.

"In someone's imaginary universe, he did," recorrected Wells.

"Cards, gentlemen," called Jules.

"I can't just sit here for ninety-six years," the youth protested.

Stephen Crane chuckled and rested his chin atop his clasped hands. "I've been here for a hundred and forty-two years."

Henry looked at his hand. He had a pair of sevens. Crane checked to Dodgson, who checked to George. George checked to Henry. The youth settled in for the long haul and threw in ten years. Baum called and Jules bumped it twenty years. Stephen, Chuck, and George folded. Henry tossed in two more chips. Frank grimaced as he shook his head. "I really shouldn't," he said as he called.

"Cards," asked Jules.

Henry kept his pair of sevens. "Three."

"Two," Baum said as he tossed his discards into the center of the table.

"And," said Jules, "the dealer takes one."

"Two pair?" asked Baum.

"We shall see."

Henry picked up his hand and squeezed the new cards out past his pair. Deuce, four . . . seven! He had trips. He tossed thirty years into the pot.

Baum folded and Jules Verne studied his hand. "Did you pick up your third card, I must ask myself." He grinned. "I think not." He counted out a hundred chips and pushed them into the center of the table. "One thousand years."

Henry trembled as he counted out his hundred chips, shoved them into the center of the table, then began counting out a thousand chips more. It would be a ten-thousand-year bet. While he was counting and trying to counter the dryness in his mouth, he heard a noise.

"Pssst!"

He looked over his shoulder, and back in the deep shadows he saw a golden visage with a white wig.

"Hugo!"

"Who's that, Henry?" asked Crane.

"That's Hugo Pissov." He looked at Stephen Crane. "Jim Conklin to you."

Crane glanced at Hugo and returned his attention to his hand. "I don't even want to hear about whatever dimension it was that produced him."

The robot gestured with his hand. "Come on, Henry. We have to go. The battle of Mt. Catastrophe is about to begin."

Henry looked back at his cards, then held them up for Hugo to see. "Look. I can win this hand—"

Hugo stepped out of the shadows and stood next to the youth. "You don't understand. Sparky and Coxey's army got to the missile control center first and we'll have to take it back from them—"

"What was your name again?" asked Baum.

"Pissov."

"Sorry."

The robot took the cards from the youth and threw them into the center of the table. "Forget it, Henry. Unless you come along right now, you'll be here forever." The metal man glanced at Chuck. "I know you. Let me see if I remember it: 'Twas Brillo in the sliding hoes, Did gyro gimbal astrolabe: all—"

"Let's go, Hugo," said Henry as he pushed away from the table and got to his feet. Chuck gathered up the chips as Hugo led Henry through dark, mist-heavy passages.

"I could have won that hand."

"What were you doing back there, brother?"

"Playing poker. It was a hell of a game."

"Those writers back there; what were they waiting for?"

"A guy named Vergil. He's supposed to guide them out of the Inferno."

"No kidding? You know, before that jerk Adolph Schwartz named me Hugo Pissov, my name was Vergil."

"Really?"

"Vergil Abominovitch. That's why I kept the name Hugo Pissov even after Schwartz was splattered all over this mortal coil." The robot paused and pointed down at a piece of black glass. "There. All we have to do is step through." The robot lifted his head about eight inches. "Look! Over there. Hah! I thought so."

"Who is it, Hugo?"

"I knew it. George Lucas." Hugo turned his volume up to maximum as he pushed Henry into the glass. Again the youth dropped into the dark as he heard Hugo's voice shouting at the hapless soul working his way down to the poker game. "Racist! R2D2 and 3CPO should have gotten medals!"

The darkness parted and the youth opened his eyes and saw the face of Anne Droid. She was lying on top of him with his member firmly in hand.

"Hi, John. Got any quarters?"

Then Hugo landed on top of both of them. Anne made a fist and swung at Hugo. Unfortunately she neglected first to let go of Henry's member. No permanent damage was done, but the screaming was quite shattering.

THIRTY-SEVEN

Loveland

SUB I-70 emptied into the huge cavern beneath the Loveland Pass just west of the Great Denver Crater. From there it would only be a few hours north to the Mt. Catastrophe Center. However, there was an army there blocking the route.

The enemy force that blocked the cavern was composed of robots and humans devoid of self-will. On a rise in the cavern floor stood the dreaded black hulk of Sparky, still holding all of the strings.

On a rise at the opposite side of the cavern stood Henry, Hugo, and General Malaise. Henry pointed at the opposing line and said to the general, "That's Coxey's Army. They've all been forced to turn traitor by Sparky."

With his flappers the general adjusted the aluminum foil wrapped around his head. "Hugo, were you able to come up with sufficient wrap to foil Sparky?"

"Yes, my son," answered the now golden robot, checking his own wrap. "I've been eating old pots and pans for hours. Look."

Below them, the assorted critters of Malaise's original command, in addition to Vicious Birdwell's force, stood at various interpretations of attention, each soldier's head wrapped in gleaming aluminum foil, each soldier's pitchfork at the ready.

The general sadly shook his head. "Hugo, couldn't you get them to use something a little more effective? Maybe bows and arrows, chain saws, slingshots?"

"Have faith, General. The boys won't let you down."

Henry pointed at Sparky. "General, our only hope is to drive straight toward that monster and pull its plug. Once that thing is out of commission, Coxey's Army will collapse."

"Do we know yet *how* to pull its plug?"

"All I need to know right now is where he is. I'll figure out the details later." Henry limped down to join Birdwell's Brigade. He walked with one hand holding his crotch and with his knees together.

Hugo followed and asked, "Why are you walking like that, brother?"

"None of your damned business."

"Where will you be, Fleming?" called the general.

"In front, carrying our banner."

"That would seem to be a very dangerous place."

"That's why I want it," answered the youth. Behind the foil-wrapped line, the youth saw Anne Droid, dressed in a Mother Hubbard outfit and holding a cased flag staff. Henry nodded at the flag staff. "Is it ready?"

"Yes, John. Are you certain you want me to wear this horrible dress?"

"Yes."

She glanced at his hand holding his heritage. A glycerine tear worked its way down her cheek. "I'm sorry about that, John. It really was an accident."

"I know."

"Hugo startled me."

"Forget it." With one arm Henry took Anne Droid by the waist and kissed her. She tenderly bit his lower lip. With his free hand the youth raised the back of her dress, located the slot, and inserted a quarter. She opened her teeth, releasing his lower lip.

"Wait for me, Anne."

"Sure, John. I'll wait for you, and only you. Come back real soon now."

Henry grabbed the cased banner. He turned to see Hugo getting his systems purged with an air pump by another robot. "Let's go, Hugo. It's time."

Hugo released the appliance, allowing Henry to see that it wore a red ballroom gown and a black wig. "Was it good for you, too, Naomi?"

"Ma?"

The robot's mouth opened into a grin. "Lord, Henry, 'tis love t' hear yer voice agin." She crushed her beer can, tossed it and her cigar butt away, and held out her arms.

Henry tossed the banner at Hugo and rushed to embrace his mother. They hugged and Henry gasped as his ribs cracked. "Ma!"

She relaxed the pressure and held her son out at arm's length. "Boy, yer lookin' right smart in thet bellhop suit."

"Ma, where'd you come from?"

"Hugo 'n' thet creepy Buggely toad brought me here through a piece o' glass." She leaned close to her son. "Boy, thet Phil Bach is one tiresome sumbitch." She looked over at the enemy forces, then back at her son.

"Yer goin' t' do me 'n' yer pappy proud t'day."

"I ran, Ma." There were tears glistening in his eyes. "In my first action, I ran."

She patted his cheek, lacerating it with a fingertip that needed deburring. "T'day yer'll do it right. I believe in yeh. Now, run 'long 'n' kick some ass."

Henry kissed his mother, took the banner back from Hugo, and stared at the metal man who had been with him through so much. The revulsion rising in the youth's chest told him the idea of Hugo for a stepfather still ran counter to every prejudice he had. Yet Hugo had changed since Henry had first met him. Now he was golden with hair of white. He no longer imbibed non-factory-specified oil, and he was a religious leader. Henry's feelings told the youth that he hadn't grown anywhere near as much as the robot had.

"Hugo, I hope you and Ma will be very happy."

"I was hoping you would say that, brother. Perhaps now I should call you son."

"Don't press it, Hugo." Henry pulled the case off the colors and unfurled the flag. It was a gleaming golden cross emblazoned on a pair of black net panties on a shining background of aluminum. Henry consigned his life and future to Mithras and Hugo drew his saber. The pair joined the center of Birdwell's ranks.

When the spaces between the stalagmites began to pour forth the masses of Coxey's Army, Henry was a bit surprised to feel, instead of terror, serene self-confidence. Blinding white beams and hissing projectiles decimated his men, but he did not duck or try to dodge whatever the fates had measured out for him. He stood erect and watched as Sparky's attack began against the left side of the line.

There was a stillness pregnant with meaning. The aluminum-capped lines of the right shifted and stared at the silent stalagmites before them. At that moment beamers hissed from the stalagmites. As the left began to retreat under the strength of Sparky's assault, the alien robot must have ordered all of Coxey's Army out onto the cavern floor in a general assault.

General Malaise raised a flapper and gave the order. The right side of the line moved out and pitchforked into Sparky's left. Henry, his banner raised, saw wild and desperate rushes of men moving backward and forward in surges. Sometimes Birdwell's men would yell and cheer, only to have their cries replaced in a second by the yells and cheers of Coxey's Army. Henry's end of the line, when once more assaulted by the enemy hordes erupted in a cry of rage and pain. Henry waved his banner and charged ahead.

"Follow me!"

"Back here, Henry," called Hugo. "It's safer back here!" Cursing an oath to Talos, Gort, and several other ancestors, Hugo leaped over the line and caught up with Henry. The men behind them, seeing the golden robot next to their banner, snarled and charged into the beamer fire.

Into the enemy left they fought, their bodies seemingly invulnerable. Henry kept the colors to the front, determined to go forward whatever the penalty. Behind him the aluminum-capped lines chewed into the enemy left like so many demons. Many of the enemy began to flee, which brought a savage, deep-throated howl of victory from Henry's side.

But at one part of the enemy line there was a hard knot of troops that refused to move. A flag, blood red and carrying an emblem of a mechanical spider, waved above them. The banner was mounted on a pole microscoping from the top of Sparky's head. Swirls of blue lightning from the black robot's head jumped and shot among the small force, keeping it in place and fighting. The soldiers of Henry's line, eyes flashing and teeth bared, launched their pitchforks at the throats of those who resisted.

Henry centered the gaze of his soul upon the enemy flag. Its possession would make up for Keynesburg General, his shattered dreams of wealth, his illicit love of the appliance Anne, all of it. If he could take that flag, he could lay it down before Mithras as evidence that his guilt was erased. He could accept his mother's stainless steel kisses as earned by a true Army son.

Henry plunged at the flag, resolved that it would not escape him should breath still be in his body. The remains of Coxey's Army loosed a volley of beamer and exploding-projectile fire, driving the aluminum caps momentarily to the rear, but the battered body of Birdwell's Brigade bolted back to the bogey barricades.

With a terrible grin of resolution, the youth hugged his own banner as his legs stumbled forward. Hugo and Henry both reached Sparky at the same time. As Henry wrenched the banner, flagpole and all, from the top of the black robot's head, Hugo clamped jumper cables from the alien's lightning antennae to his horns, shorting him out.

At that moment the battle ended. The remains of Coxey's Army woke up and began inquiring where they were. None of them remembered anything since Keynesburg. Birdwell's Brigade took them in and began dressing their wounds.

Henry stood next to the black robot, holding the alien's flag over its deenergized carcass. The red and black fabric fluttered slowly.

Hugo removed his wig in respect and said, "Rust in peace, Sparky."

THIRTY-EIGHT

Maybe It Is
All Just a Dream

THE Mt. Catastrophe Ultimate Retaliation Control Center
was a huge cavern illuminated by three dim emergency
lights. High, up near the ceiling, was mounted a ring of
enormous display screens, now blank and lifeless. Four decades of dust coated the floors, maintaining a record of generations of mouse and roach migrations. The sounds of the
adventurers were muffled by curtains of cobwebs.

"It's all set," said General Malaise.

Henry looked toward the back of the cavern and saw the
general standing before a console, a tear in his eye. "General?"

"It's just like it was that day in '99 when the White House
ordered the strike shut down." He held out his flappers.
"Barely two hundred missiles had been launched when the
shutdown was ordered. There were twenty-six thousand
more missiles rarin' to go, but the plug was pulled."

The youth stood next to General Malaise and looked down
at the console. He could make no sense at all out of the maze
of dials, switches, knobs, and indicators. "What was it you
said about it being all set? All set for what?"

"Why, boy, we shut down right in the middle of everything. No check lists, no graded stand-down, no replacement of safety interlocks, no nothin'. The retaliatory strike was put on pause and the power was pulled."

"Do you mean we actually could launch a devastating strike against the Soviet economic machine?"

"Yes. Why, son, we could pick up right where we left off if we could just get a few miserable electrons to power the equipment."

"General, we're only here to threaten Ivan. We're not here to end life on earth as we know it."

"Of course, Fleming. But for any kind of threat to be effective, we need to be able to back it up with the possibility of the real thing." He pointed a flapper at a row of consoles and cabinets. "That's Glass Nose Row. It's a sophisticated monitoring system put in as a result of the mutual-missile-sniffing peace initiatives decades ago. As soon as we crank up the center, this system will ring every bell in the Kremlin."

The lights went on accompanied by the whines and whirs of countless air recirculation fans. "Ah," said the general, "power." He motioned to his men. "Man the strike boards." He turned to Henry. "It looks as though your troops have finally gotten the generators working."

A small army of automatic cleaning robots shot out from the walls and began attacking the dust and dead bugs. Hugo, Ma, Anne, and Grunt Buggely walked up to General Malaise and Henry. Hugo patted Grunt Buggely on his head. "It took a little magic, but we got the generators going."

"General Malaise," called the crab with the human hands for legs.

"Yes, Windrush?"

"Sir, the firing board isn't manned."

"Well, where's Colonel Musk? That's his station." At the silence his question drew, the general put his flappers on his hips intending to make cakes out of the crab. "Where is Colonel M—" He nodded as memory finally served. ". . . the Lobster Newburg." He faced Hugo and pointed at one of the stations. "Sit there so that the monitor can read that the station is manned."

"Yes, my son," said the golden robot.

"Don't touch anything."

"Lighten up, General. I'm programmed for this kind of stuff."

Hugo lowered himself into the chair and the moment his can touched the seat, banks of lights illuminated on Glass Nose Row.

The general pointed at the red telephone at one of the Glass Nose stations. "Maybe another five seconds—" The phone began ringing. The general saluted with a flapper. "See?"

Henry nodded and reached over to pick up the receiver. "Hello?"

The guttural voice at the other end was very angry. "Hello, you say? Hello?"

Henry sat on the edge of the nearest console. "Yes, I said hello. Is there something I can do for you?"

"What madman is giving orders there in America? Our equipment says you are preparing to launch an all-out nuclear strike. Is that true?"

"Strangely enough, that's what our equipment says, too, Ivan."

"Are you insane, American pig—"

Henry turned to Hugo. "This guy talks just like you."

"—have nothing but borscht for brains? Don't you know what could happen—"

"I'll tell you what can happen," interrupted Henry. "If your companies don't knock off the competition in Europe, if they don't simply pack up and clear out, thousands of nuclear weapons will turn the Soviet Union into one large Chernobyl." He nodded at Hugo. "Sign off."

"Sign off," repeated the metal man as he punched a button cutting off the connection.

Henry hung up the phone and leaned against a console. "What should we do while we're letting them stew, General?"

"A lot has changed since The Last War. We should show some retargeting activity, particularly concentrating on their newest industrial centers." The general poked Hugo's shoulder with a flapper. "Are you really programmed for that kind of board?"

"Sure. Just tell me what you want me to do."

"Excellent." The general walked up a set of steps to a row of consoles overlooking the rest of the room. "It'll take me a minute to get this cranked up. Put on your headset."

"What headset? I don't have one."

"Neither do I, General," called out the handy crab.

Henry waved his hand. "General, just call out your orders to me and I'll relay them."

"Very well, but it's a hell of a way to save a railroad. Energize the main screens."

"Energize the main screens," repeated Henry.

"Energize main screens," said Hugo, flipping a bank of ganged switches. The row of huge screens circling the ceiling of the cavern began to glow. Every country on earth was depicted as maps. Additional screens showed satelite transmissions, while still additional ones showed enlargements of map and photo sections.

Anne Droid stood next to Henry and hugged him. "I'm so proud of you, John."

"I yam too, son. Y' done yer pappy 'n' me proud."

He held his two girls by the waist and looked down at the wizard. "Grunt Buggely, one thing that would make this moment just perfect is if I could share it with my friend Sergeant Major Boyle. We lost him at the same time we lost Anne and my Ma, along with two others. Do you think you could use your glass and bring him back?"

"Humph. I'm a wizard, aren't I? I could bring all three if I put my mind to it."

"Johnny Morgan and Harry?"

"I said so, didn't I?" Buggely turned and walked from the cavern to get his equipment.

"Odessa sectional chart," called out the general.

"Odessa sectional chart," repeated Henry.

"Odessa sectional chart," answered Hugo as he typed a code into his keyboard. As soon as he did so an enlargement of part of the Soviet Union appeared on the screen.

"Update industrial scan," called out the general.

"Update industrial scan," repeated Henry.

"Update industrial scan," answered Windrush.

A red line appeared on the screen and began sweeping back and forth across the image from the bottom to the top.

Every now and then it would leave a bright yellow dot behind. The general would order up a particular missile or series of missiles, Henry would repeat the order, Windrush would prepare the missiles for retargeting, the general would order the birds retargeted, Henry would repeat the order, and Hugo would answer as he positioned the retargeting cursor over the new target and locked it in. After a few minutes of this, Glass Nose Row's red telephone rang. Henry picked up the receiver. "Hello?"

"This is Marshal Karpoff, commander of the Doomsday center. Who am I speaking with?"

"Henry Fleming."

"What is your title?"

"Cadet sergeant."

"What?" There was a shouted string of unfamiliar phrases, then Karpoff was back on the line. "Fleming?"

"Yes?"

"What is all of this nonsense about blowing up the Union of Soviet Socialist Republics unless we cripple our European trade?"

"You said it very well, Marshal Karpoff. If you need it said simpler: get out of Europe or we turn you into glass."

"Are you insane? Is everyone in America mad? If you fired missiles at us, we'd have to fire them back at you. How many times has the world heard Sagan's message about the dreaded Nuclear Winter?"

"Billyions and billyions," Henry confirmed. "Nevertheless, if we lost the competition, there wouldn't be much point in living anyway, would there? So get out of Europe, Marshal Karpoff, or we shoot."

There was a long silence from the other end. At last Marshal Karpoff spoke. "I will get back to you in a short while, Henry Fleming."

"Good-bye, Marshal Karpoff." Henry hung up the telephone.

General Malaise called down from his station. "What happened?"

Henry folded his arms and grinned. "I think the other guy just blinked."

Hugo howled and a small, but lusty, cheer made its way

around the cavern. "Let's keep up the retargeting activity," said the general, "so they don't think we were just bluffing. Call up the Kiev sectional chart."

Henry repeated the order, and Hugo answered as he made the entry. They called up two more charts, scanned them for updates, and retargeted their assigned missiles. They were just beginning a new chart as Henry thought he saw something at the entrance to the cavern.

"Kharkov sectional chart," the general called out.

"Kharkov sectional chart," repeated Henry as he saw his Ma and Anne enter the cavern with Grunt Buggely.

"Kharkov sectional chart," answered Hugo as he punched it up on the screen.

Another figure entered the cavern wearing red brassiere and panties. He carried a book under one arm and a giant stuffed panda under the other.

"Harry! Harry Nucome," Henry shouted.

"Hurry, nuke 'em," repeated Hugo as he unlocked a red switch and threw it.

Henry turned to the robot and stared it in the sensors. "Not 'hurry.' *Harry*. Harry Nucome. N-u-c-o-m-e. Nucome."

"Oops."

"Oops? *Oops?* What do you mean, oops?"

"My mistake. Sorry."

Henry looked up to see the missile tracks beginning to make their map marks on their way to destroy a hemisphere. There were more tracks being put down by Russian missiles as they headed on their way to destroy the remaining hemisphere. The youth looked up at General Malaise.

"It's no use, son." The general threw up his flappers. "The safety destruct panels don't work. Something must be burnt out. It's no use."

Henry sat down on the floor. It seemed to be a proper place from which to observe the end of the world. Harry Nucome sat down next to the youth.

"Y' know, Henry," said Harry, "for me it began in Wayne State University in Detroit back when I was teaching bonehead economics to a bunch of freshmen who couldn't care less. To keep myself from going to sleep, I used to tape my lectures. Once my equipment was running, I'd leave the hall and go back to my office and work while the students listened to the tape and took notes."

Harry twitched. "One time in my office I couldn't find my pen—the silver one inscribed with my name. I returned to the lecture hall to see if I had left it there. Because it was right in the middle of the tape, I sneaked in so as not to disturb anyone. When I reached the lectern and found my pen, I looked out at the students and witnessed something. *There were no students in the hall*. Instead, at each desk was a tape recorder taking down the lecture that *my* tape recorder was delivering."

He reached out a hand and grasped Henry's arm. "Don't you see it? We had machines that recorded and stored the content—the data—in my lectures, and more machines that could interpret, digest, and implement the information. The process no longer required the presence of humans! We were nothing but superfluous protoplasm."

Harry released Henry's arm and slowly shook his head. "The next thing I knew I was in a rubber room at Jung-Edison, wearing red panties and a bra, reading Samuelson to a stuffed panda."

"Everything seemed to be going so well for a minute," said Henry, all emotion ironed from his voice. He held his fingertips to his temples as he began feeling light-headed and dizzy. "I think . . . I think I'm going to pass out." He grabbed Harry's arm as he whispered, "Thank Sherman, it's a dream. It really is all just a dream."

The cavern went dark and Henry, his heart freed from this reality, cheered to a deaf universe.

Stephen Crane awakened and shouted to his darkened room, "I've got it! *The Rust Badge of Courage!*"

THIRTY-NINE

Grave New World

"**M**Y Brother wanted to be a robot mechanic, but he fainted at the sight of oil."

"Gaa, guh duh, bi-bi," the youth responded. He couldn't seem to get his lips to move.

"That was a joke."

"Goo goo, da da, poo poo, ca ca."

The voice came from so far away it wasn't even there. Instead there was the eternal delicious hiss, a strange dryness in the throat, a high-pitched squeal, a thing slurping beneath his tongue. It was once again time to reconsider the problem of radio protocol. He was considering the roger-wilco event.

Say an airplane reports to a control tower that the flight is in trouble. It is important for the tower to know when the transmission is concluded, which is why the pilot ends his transmission with the word "over." It is just as important, however, for the pilot to know that the tower received and understood the transmission he sent. This is why the tower incorporates the word "roger" in its message. It is equally important for the tower to know that its roger has been received and understood, otherwise it would have to be sent again. But how does the tower know that the pilot has received the tower's roger? The pilot incorporates the term "wilco" in its return transmission.

But, posited the youth, is it not just as important for the pilot to know that the tower has received and understood the airplane's wilco? Of course it is, which is why the tower should return with "wilco understood," or, perhaps, "roger your wilco." But what if the pilot never received the tower's roger of his wilco? The only way the tower can be sure is if the pilot acknowledges the transmission with, oh, say, "roger your roger of my wilco," or something of the sort.

Yet we are still faced with the remaining problem that can only be resolved by the tower rogering the pilot's roger of the tower's roger of the pilot's wilco. And still, there . . .

He felt something lift from his nose. A mask. Roger the mask. Wilco. Roger your wilco. Roger your roger of my wilco. Roger your—

A mask, thought the youth. A mask! Nitrous oxide! It was a dream! Oh, bliss. I did go to the dentist's office. I didn't enlist in the Economy. Oh, thank Caesar!

He felt with his tongue and found to his surprise that his bridge was missing. In addition there seemed to be upward of about fifty sharp-edged holes in his teeth.

Henry opened his eyes, and he was indeed in a dentist's office. However, it looked different from the Army's facility at Ft. Calley. There was activity outside his field of vision, and he didn't appear yet to have motor control over his neck muscles. He could see the sky through the room's lone window, and it was cloudy. There was an advertising shingle mounted outside that Henry could see through the window and he forced his eyes to focus on its printed words. It read: "Stan S. Fluoride, Dedicated Dentalbot."

The doctor's metal face rolled back into view as the orthodonotron's suction appendage was withdrawn from Henry's mouth. "There, you're all finished, Mr. Fleming. All of your old fillings have been drilled out." The dentalbot ejected the drill bits from the tips of his fingers. "Are you certain you don't want me to fill them for you?"

"No. Don't fill them. I don't want any artificial parts." There was memory and Henry drew his palm over his bald head. All of his hair had fallen out. There were horrible sores on the back of his hand, and his body stank of rotted meat. He was at the new ski resort in San Torqué.

"I wouldn't charge anything. I mean it's a real privilege to work on living teeth again." Dr. Fluoride removed the bib from Henry's neck. "Do you mind if I share something with you?"

Henry sat up, his elbows leaning on the chair's armrests. "No. Go ahead."

"Thank you. You see, I'm a dedicated dentalbot. I'm only programmed for one thing: dentistry. Now, some of the classier androids have teeth, but they never need work. I'm dedicated to working on human teeth."

"What's your point, Stan?"

"The point? The point is that you're the last living human on earth. Do you have any idea what I have had to do to try and find patients upon which to use my skills?"

Henry moved his legs off of the footrest and swung them gingerly to the floor. "Get a new package."

"But then I wouldn't be me. I'd be wiped and loaded with who knows what."

"I don't know what to tell you." Henry smiled a bit. "Except hit the graveyards." With a great effort, the youth pushed himself to his feet.

"Graveyards?"

"Sure. They're filled with bodies that have teeth with all kinds of dental problems. Dig 'em up, drill 'em, fill 'em, and bury 'em again. There should be enough work to keep you busy until Hell thaws out."

"I never even thought of that before." Stan S. Fluoride's video sensors wandered out of sync as he pondered the glorious treasure beneath the surface of the earth. "It would cost more, having them dug up, transported, making certain that all of the odd little bits and pieces were picked up. But I could save a fortune on anesthetics, antiseptics, magazines. And how much easier it would be on my back. I wouldn't have to scrunch down and go into all kinds of contortions trying to drill and fill an upper mandible. A loose skull you can flip around any old way. I could even remove the lower mandible, making everything easy to get at."

Henry began walking from the room when Dr. Fluoride

extended an arm and halted him. "Thank you, Mr. Fleming, for your suggestion. You are an absolute saint."

"Don't mention it."

"You've saved my life. Perhaps I can return the favor."

"How?"

"Well, I can see what kind of condition you're in. It's amazing you've managed to survive for as long as you have."

"Magic," said the youth as a fleeting memory of Grunt Buggely passed behind his eyes.

"In any event," continued the dentalbot, "every single part of you that is failing right now can be replaced. Robobiotronics is a very advanced science. They can do miracles."

"It's not for me. I don't want any artificial parts."

"That's very narrow-minded, Mr. Fleming."

"Nevertheless."

"Very well. Thank you again, and take care."

Henry walked from the room. As he was paying his bill, the receptiotron played a telephone message: "Henry, this 's yer Ma. I jes' wanted t' tell yer that Hugo called 'n' 's lookin' fer yer. Anyway, c'mon over 'n' give yer Ma a big kiss, 'n' I got somethin' I made up fer ye."

Henry pulled his overcoat collar up against the June cold as he slogged through the snow toward San Torqué's municipal cemetery. If Stan S. Fluoride would be digging up bodies, the youth figured he had best check up on the security arrangements he had made.

The wind howled, sending a wave of mad clicking across the town as toy Geiger counters went off in every household. Henry glanced up at the boiling dark clouds and figured that the new snowstorm announced on the news would materialize after all.

"Doesn't seem like there's anyplace left to put it." At least, he thought, it will freshen up the slopes for the skibots.

On the distant snow-covered mountain whose bowels contained the remains of the Ultimate Retaliation Control Center, he could see lights moving. They were skiers rapidly getting in their pleasure before the opening of the Summer Olympics on Monday. Near the Bijou Theater a Mark Eight ski instructor was taking his teeniebopperbot date to the movies. Henry glanced at the marquee to see what was playing: "The Terminator—Surprise Ending!"

Red-painted Santatrons were on their corners, ringing their bells, wishing everyone season's greetings. In a department store window was a robot reading a holiday story to a group of toddlerbots. Above the cardboard mantelpiece hung with stockings was a quotation: "And Shiny Tim said 'Gort bless us, every one.'"

With snow all year around, the marketing computers quickly made the Christmas buying season a twelve-month event. The world was prosperous and at peace, something certain alien presences did not miss, and which they communicated to the Galactic League of Worlds.

The youth entered the cemetery and noticed that the resting place's Torotrons were lubing up to clear the paths during the coming storm. He halted at the fenced-in plot where he and Ma had put Sergeant Major Boyle to his final rest. A huge roboticized snake was coiled atop the grave, seemingly sound asleep. Henry was wroth.

"Wake up! You, wake up!"

"Eh?"

"Wake up! How are you going to frighten anyone like that?"

"I'm here, aren't I?"

"Look, either hiss or get off the plot!"

When Henry left, the snake was putting on a fairly effective display of frightening moves. If the moves were sufficient to ward off a desperate dentalbot Henry didn't know. Anyway, thought the lad, maybe the Old Soldier could stand to get his teeth done. He certainly couldn't afford it when he was alive.

At his mother's house the youth sat and watched as Ma Pissov knitted baby clothes out of steel wool.

"Yer a sight, Henry, 'n' there's no gittin' round it. I respect yer 'pinions 'bout artificial parts 'n' all, but yer could do with a bit o' deodorant."

"That's artificial, too, Ma."

"I know, I know." She crushed her beer can and tossed it

across the room. "Seems a shame, though. Fine-lookin' boy like yerself. What 'bout Anne? Think she likes t' have yer stinkin' up t' place? 'Tain't so easy t' clean, now thet yer leavin' little bits o' yerself here 'n' there."

"My mind's made up, Ma."

She sighed, shook her head, and rattled her copper curls. "Here's yer mail." She gave him a heavily padded envelope. The return address was from Merrill Lynch Honda in Piscataway, New Jersey. Henry tore open the envelope and four sets of keys and some credit cards fell out of the envelope onto the floor. He picked them up. There was a letter inside, and Henry read it.

Merrill Lynch Honda
101 Currency Ave.,
Piscataway, NJ 08854

To: Henry Fleming,
c/o Hugo and Naomi Pissov
227 Ellison Blvd.,
San Torqué, CO 80537

My Dear Henry,

I am pleased and personally honored to be the one to inform you that you have been unanimously elected chairman of the board of the Merrill Lynch Honda worldwide family of industries.

Enclosed please find your keys to the executive washroom, your membership card and key to the worldwide chain of Fondlebunny Clubs, the keys to your company car, and your keys to your company jet. In addition, please find the current copy of our corporation report.

Again, warmest congratulations, and please accept my personal good wishes for a successful term of office.

Most cordially,

He handed the letter to his mother. "What do you think of that, Ma?"

She began reading the letter and Henry picked up the report and leafed through the lists of Merrill Lynch Honda holdings. There was every kind of enterprise from genetic engineering to video games. Ma Fleming squeaked with glee and clanged her hands together. "I knowed yer'd make it, Henry. I jest knowed it. Y' done me 'n' yer pappy proud."

Henry looked again at the letter. "It's not signed."

"'Course not. Thet kind o' computer only writes 'n' types. It cain't sign nothin'."

"Ma, it won't mean anything unless it's signed."

"Sign it yerself then. Yer t' onlyest human employee of thet comp'ny. Yer entitled."

"It's not going to be much, with me the only employee."

"Chairman of the board? Hit's a livin', Henry, 'n' it'll be yards better'n that job yer got over t' t' museum."

"You're right there, Ma." He pulled a pen out of his pocket and signed the letter.

"My congrats, Henry."

"Thanks. I gotta go." He bent over, kissed her cheek, and stood up. "Did Hugo leave a message?"

"I wish you'd call 'im pa, daddy, father, or somethin'. He'd really like thet."

"What about the message?"

She reached out, picked up a slip of paper from her knitting basket, and handed it to her son. "I don't want yer two t' git int' fightin' now, hear?"

"Sure, Ma." The note from Hugo read:

> Dear Henry,
>> Meet me at the Wheatstone Bridge,
>>> Hugo.

"I wonder what he wants." He tucked the message into his overcoat pocket, just barely noticing that the pinky finger on his right hand was missing. "Ma, in your message you said you had something for me."

"Why, fer goodness sake, I plumb fergot all 'bout it." She

rummaged around for a moment, then snapped her fingers with a sound resembling a rat trap. "I remember. I gave it t' Hugo t' give to yer."

Henry bent over and kissed her cheek, cutting himself on a rough edge. He noticed, however, that his lip did not bleed. Things had been dropping off for days, but there had been no bleeding. He didn't even seem to have a pulse. "Ma, you really ought to have those rough edges deburred."

"So long, Henry."

"'Bye, Ma." The youth left his mother's house, the letter of notification in his hand. Chairman of the board of Merrill Lynch Honda, he thought. He saw a telephone booth and headed for it. Picking up the receiver, Henry patted his pockets trying to find a quarter. He was, as usual, all out.

"Operator," said the receiver.

"I'm sorry," said Henry, "but it appears that I am all out of change."

"Would you care to place a collect call, Chairman Fleming?"

"How . . . how did you know my name?"

The operator snorted out a laugh that sounded like a cross between a mule braying and a hog oinking. "Goodness gracious, you silly pudding, no one else is left."

"Do you think Merrill Lynch Honda would accept a collect call from me?"

"You, Henry Fleming, are the chairman of the board. You're damned right they'll accept the charges. If they don't, I'll cut out their phone service for a year." That laugh again. Somehow it reminded the youth of the Inferno.

"Merrill Lynch Honda," answered a synthesized voice.

"This is Chairman Fleming. Give me personnel."

"Yes sir, Mr. Fleming."

There was a buzz, then another voice. "Personnel."

"This is Chairman Fleming."

"Yes sir, Mr. Fleming. What can I do for you?"

"Do you have an android named Arnold on the payroll?"

"We have several, sir. Do you have a surname?"

"No. The one I have in mind does company recruiting in Ft. Calley, Texas."

"Yes, Mr. Fleming. Arnold 44B."

"Good," said Henry as he thanked Mithras for small favors. "Scrap him."

"Do you mean let him go, sir?"

"No. One of our holdings is Hormel-Frisky, right?"

"Yes sir."

"Transfer him there and have him stamped into catfood cans. Got that?"

"Yes *sir*! Is there anything else, sir?"

"That's it." The youth hung up the receiver and hailed a taxi. "The museum, and step on it."

FORTY

A Snowball's Chance

HENRY Went to his display case at the San Torqué Museum of Natural History and gathered up his things. There wasn't much besides his glasses, his copy of Samuelson, and his giant panda.

"Where're you goin' now, lad, eh?"

Henry looked at Harrison, the curatorbot. "I'm quitting."

"See here, you can't quit."

"It's a free country."

"Of course, lad, of course it is. But don't you see, we can't replace you. You're one of a kind."

"I'm sorry."

"If it's a matter of more quarters—"

"It's not that. I've just been made chairman of the board at Merrill Lynch Honda."

"Well!" Harrison folded his arms and flashed a cold video sensor at Henry. "Would it be too much to ask that you notify your supervisor before you go?"

"I was going to do that."

The curatorbot huffed off as Henry closed the display case, hefted his book and panda, and headed toward the Automata Hall of Fame to search for Phil Bach. The youth figured Phil ought to be near the end of his tour by now. As he approached, Henry could see the small crowd of robots listening to Phil's lecture. Phil stood upon a slightly raised platform. Behind him on the wall was a frieze of a golden robot that looked a lot like 3CPO with a bit of the new Hugo thrown in here and there. Next to it was painted a famous quotation:

> I have created a machine
> in the image of man,
> that never tires or makes
> a mistake.
> —Rotwang the Inventor
> Fritz Lang's *Metropolis*, 1925

"... From legend," Phil continued, "we have Talos, the metal man who guarded the island of Crete. It was built by Daedalus for King Minos. Such guard robots were the mythical ancestors of the V1 and V2, and the Cruise missiles." He pointed toward a model of a horrible rocklike creature. "Also from legend is the Golem, supposedly molded from clay. Golem is the ancestor of Jewish robotry. It was brought to life by inserting the *shem* into its mouth. Obviously the *shem* is a program."

Phil aimed his pointer light at what appeared to be a bucket of monkey snot. "The ancestor of the androids, of course, is this early attempt of the alchemist Albertus Magnus to build his *androides* in 1727. And, moving on, we have Frankenstein's so-called monster, Rudy. He ..."

As Henry half listened, a thought crept into his mind. The tour moved on, but the youth remained in front of the bucket of monkey snot. He was certain he had seen it listed in the corporation's holdings. He rapidly leafed through the report —there! Genentech-Birdseye Sperm and Egg Banks. He read the description, and it was all there. Once Sagan's Spring came, melting away the radioactive snow, the human race could be reborn. Fertilized human egg cells could be implanted and attached to—

He thought again, for there were no more horses, cows, bears, or gorillas.

Henry scratched his head, thereby removing several centimeters of flesh. He needed mammals large enough to hold a human embryo to term, but nothing that large was left. Mice, moles, a few privately held hamsters.

His newly born hope waning, he absentmindedly paged through the rest of the corporation's frozen assets: King Kut–Dairy Queen Soft Frozen Dog Food, Popsicle-Trojan Freeze-Dried Condoms, Forest Lawn–Pepperidge Farm Cryogenic Interments—

The youth looked over the description of Forest Lawn–Pepperidge Farm. "There are hundreds and hundreds of living humans. They're all sick one way or another, but there must be enough females that can keep it kicking long enough to—"

Wait, thought Henry. What if Forest Lawn–Pepperidge Farm bought it along with most of the rest of the world? "Of course, it wouldn't be in the report if it had been wiped." He found a telephone and called to make certain. It was true. The main branch of the facility was located deep inside a huge Maine salt mine. Just to make doubly sure, he placed a call to the international headquarters of Forest Lawn–Pepperidge Farm Cryogenic Interments, Farmington, Maine.

The robot on the other end of the line was a Mark Seven Eastleratron named Autotom. He assured Henry that the facility was still in operation, was in perfect running order, and that the horizontal population stood at 226,904.

"Thank you very much, Autotom."

"Mr. Fleming, just one thing."

"Yes?"

"Well, as the chairman of Merrill Lynch Honda, you should be able either to confirm or deny a rumor we've had running around here for some time."

"I will if I can. What is it?"

"What with the long winter and all, it's been speculated that a large conglomerate, such as Merrill Lynch Honda, might start up the earmuff factory again."

"Earmuffs?"

"That's right. The inventor of the earmuff, Chester Greenwood, lived here and had his factory here."

"I didn't think robots had ears. At least ears that got cold."

"Well, sir, they don't. For us the earmuff factory is a sentimental matter rather than——"

"Look, Autotom," interrupted the youth, "I can't deal with this right now, but I'll get back to you as soon as I can. Good-bye."

"Good-bye, Mr. Fleming."

Just before he hung up the phone, Henry heard the Farmington robot holler, "Beverly. Tell Larry to forget it."

Leaving his belongings behind, Henry headed for the street. It was time to talk to Hugo.

FORTY-ONE

Our Lady of
Perpetual Motion

T HE Wheatstone Bridge was located in a garden at St.
Catherine's Spiritual Retreat in the industrial R.U.R.
Valley west of San Torqué. Since he was broke, Henry
had to walk most of the way. Only at the last was he able to
hitch a ride with an automated Mack long-hauler. He
thanked the computer, stepped down, and faced St. Catherine's.

On the front of the massive cathedral was an automated
Catherine Wheel complete with automated Catherine. The
robotic saint, tied hand and foot to the wheel, continually
rotated until it reached an automatic arm and sword where
her head was cut off. The head would fall into a basket and
the body would rotate around, the neck bleeding white fluid
instead of blood, proving that she had been a Hyperdyne
Systems 120-A2 Android instead of a human. The body
would rotate farther until it reached the top where her head
was miraculously reattached and the cycle was repeated.

Henry passed through the huge doors and entered a softly
illuminated vestibule. A Mark Three nundroid rolled up and
stopped before him. "May I help you?" The nundroid's
video sensors gleamed brightly. "I remember you. You're
Fleming Henry."

Henry looked closely. "Gredel Ratchet?"

"I'm Sister Automatia now."

"How've you been?"

"I took my vows after Sparky passed on to his reward."

"There'll never be another like him."

"How true," said Sister Automatia, "how true. Have you come to see Hugo?"

"Yes. Is he in the garden?"

She shoved a disk into Henry's mouth and said, "Follow your program, my son." She wheeled off into a side chapel.

Henry spat out the disk along with three teeth and a bit of his tongue. Leaving his pieces on the carpet, Henry turned to his left and headed through the doors into the garden. The golden robot would be on the bridge, looking at the view of Mt. Catastrophe, meditating.

Standing in the open doorway, Henry knocked softly and peeked into the garden. As he had expected, the robot was in the center of the bridge. Henry noticed that one of his own fingers had come off on the door. He plucked it off and stuffed it into his pocket as he stepped down into the garden and walked to the bridge. Hugo was seated cross-legged, floating three feet above the deck, meditating.

"Ohm, Ohm, Ohm . . ." Hugo's video sensors energized and he turned his head. "Brother Fleming."

"Yes, Hugo. I've come to see you about something important."

Hugo lowered himself to the bridge's surface, uncrossed his legs, and stood up. "What can I do for you?"

"Do you remember when you were on trial for stealing the Queen of Hearts' parts?"

Hugo folded his arms. "Yes. I remember."

"And my testimony got you off. Do you remember that?"

"Get to the point, Brother Fleming."

Henry pulled the Merrill Lynch Honda report out of his overcoat pocket. "Look at this, Hugo. Genentech-Birdseye has hundreds of millions of sperm and egg cells in deep freeze, and over here"—Henry flipped the page—"Forest Lawn–Pepperidge Farm has thousands of humans in cryogenic suspension." He looked up at the golden robot.

Hugo turned his video sensors toward the mountains. "What's your point, brother?"

"It's plain as the nose on—well, you don't have a nose—"

"Neither do you."

Henry felt with his remaining fingers and confirmed the robot's observation. "Anyway, the human race isn't dead, Hugo. We can resurrect it."

Hugo stared silently at the mountains for a long time. He turned his face toward Henry and said, "No. That would be taking a step backward."

"Backward! Why you refugee from a junkyard, if it wasn't for me you'd still be out flat on a field in Keynesburg, your pan sucked dry." Henry turned his back on the robot. Looking into Hugo's office he could see their trophy, Sparky's banner, hung on the wall. "You said you didn't want the robots to take over."

"Brother, I said I didn't want the *alien* robots to take over." He placed a hand on Henry's shoulder. "Besides, Henry, the robots haven't taken over; humanity has evolved."

"What?"

"Humanity has taken an evolutionary jump. It has adapted to the environment. Why should we try to recreate a race that set up this time bomb and that can no longer live here now that it's been set off?"

"Once the skies clear and the radiation is washed away, Hugo, humans can live here again. You could put things in motion to make that happen."

"Humans *are* living here, Henry. They're made of metal, plastic, biomold, and Royalex, but they're human all the same."

Henry thought for a moment in silence. He was going about this all wrong. He stood behind Hugo, placed his hands on the robot's shoulders, and pointed at the mountains. "Try and see the great cities and industrial complexes we used to have, Hugo. Once all of the wills have been probated, those people in cryogenic suspension will be very, very wealthy. Can you imagine how they would regard you, the savior of the human race? All of the money you could imagine, power, fame, love, little girls—endless rivers of Addix—"

"Get thee hence, *sapiens*!" cried Hugo.

The robot ran around Henry into his office and Henry was crestfallen. In fact he was really crestfallen, his forehead having fallen on the deck. He bent over to pick it up, but a golden hand reached the flap of skin first. Hugo picked it up and handed it back to Henry as he led the youth into his office.

"Brother Fleming, you've got to pull yourself together."

Henry took the skin and put it into his pocket. "I know. Lately I've been going to pieces."

"It's too bad Grunt Buggely couldn't give you another treatment before he took the black glass to wherever."

Henry sighed and shrugged his shoulders as he dropped the corporation report on Hugo's desk. "Well, I tried. By the way, Ma said she gave you something for me."

"Of course," said Hugo. "I had forgotten all about it." The robot walked to his desk, opened the drawer, and withdrew a slender instrument. It was a quarter welded on its edge to a piece of wire coat hanger. "It's from your mother and me both."

Henry turned the instrument over in his hands and almost felt like crying. "I know you must have suggested this. It's very thoughtful." The youth paused as he fought to get out the word. "Thanks, Dad."

Before going home, Henry bought Anne a box of assorted nuts. That night, after a session of lovemaking that only the greatest gods could have imagined, Henry lay on his back staring at the luscious twin mounds of Anne Droid's behind.

Thought he, You sort of wonder about the scientists and technicians who designed and built something like Anne. How many dirty fingers had stolen into her intimate zones before she had been energized and could defend herself. He moved the remains of his left hand over her buttocks, thinking that perhaps Hugo was right. Maybe the robots hadn't

...en over. Perhaps humanity had just evolved to become something better, stronger, more noble.

"Well," he whispered to himself, "there's not much point in losing sleep over it." He unscrewed the top of his head, dropped his brain into the bowl of Eferment, and settled down for a long winter's nap.

NOTE

On April first, in the year of our Messiahbot
Hugo Pissov 2999, Henry Fleming was officially
canonized by the pontifbot, Pope Machinamentum XII.